MW00878263

RESCUE!

RESCUE!

VICTOR KELLEHER

DIAL BOOKS
New York

First published in the United States 1992 by Dial Books
A Division of Penguin Books USA Inc.
375 Hudson Street · New York, New York 10014

Published in Australia 1985 by Viking Kestrel,
an imprint of Penguin Books Australia Ltd.
Copyright © 1985 by Victor Kelleher
All rights reserved
Design by Ann Finnell
Printed in U.S.A.
1 3 5 7 9 10 8 6 4 2

Library of Congress Cataloging in Publication Data
Kelleher, Victor, 1939–
Rescue! an african adventure / Victor Kelleher.
p.   cm.
Summary: After freeing two ailing baboons from
a research station in Africa, David and Jess are unexpectedly
caught up in a struggle for survival in the bush.
ISBN 0-8037-0900-5
[1. Africa—Fiction.   2. Survival—Fiction.
3. Baboons—Fiction.   4. Animals—Treatment—Fiction.]
I. Title.
PZ7.K28127Re   1992   [Fic]—dc20   91-30490   CIP   AC

*I wish to express my sincere gratitude to the
Literature Board of the Australia Council
whose kind assistance enabled me
to complete this book.*

ONE

He could hear nothing while the storm lasted, everything blotted out by the steady drumming of the rain on the iron roof. When it stopped, there was a brief silence broken only by the soft whisper of water running along the gutters. He waited, and at the first light puff of wind a smell of damp earth drifted through the screened window of the room, followed soon afterward by the rising clamor of insect life as the normal sounds of the African night resumed. He picked up his pen, intending to continue with the essay that lay unfinished on the desk before him. It was then that he heard it: a single hoarse bark that carried clearly across the night to where he sat; a noise that, to his ears, conveyed an unmistakable note of unease and fear.

Instantly he was on his feet, listening intently, his youthful face drawn into an anxious frown. The bark was not repeated. Instead there was a cry that he knew equally well: a kind of yak-yak-yak, shrill and unhappy. Involuntarily, he pictured the face behind it: the thrusting snout, the mouth half open, the lips drawn back from strong teeth. The same cry came again, seemingly directed straight at him, and without hesitation he hurried from his room.

It was much cooler outside, and very dark, the stars and moon obscured by cloud. Pausing only long enough to get his bearings, he stumbled over to the line of mango trees that led straight down the slope. Beneath their canopy of glossy leaves it was even darker, and he had to feel his way from trunk to trunk, relying completely on the trees to guide him. At regular intervals the uneasy bark or the sharp yakking noise was repeated, as though calling specifically to him. Despite the darkness he quickened his pace, his feet swishing through the short, wet grass.

A minute or two later he emerged from beneath the trees near the bottom of the slope. His eyes had accustomed themselves now to the darkness, so that he could easily make out the square silvery structure of the large outer cage. The small inner cages, sitting high on their stands, were at first merely blurred outlines. But with his face pressed against the outer mesh these too became clearer.

"Papio," he whispered.

There was an answering grunt from the nearest of the many cages, and a dark shape moved inside it, apparently uncoiling itself from the background shadows. Even in the poor light David was able to distinguish the heavy head, the familiar flash of silver as the face turned in his direction. When a portion of the shape seemed to detach itself from the rest, he forced his hand between the mesh and returned the gentle pressure of the proffered fingers. That contact alone was enough to reassure him. As if to put him further at ease, the low grunt was repeated—a warm, friendly sound that conveyed no hint of the fear he had detected in the earlier cries.

2

Carefully, he disengaged his hand and withdrew his arm.

"Sleep now, Papio," he said, "sleep."

The dark figure obediently settled back, and David edged along until he was opposite another of the inner cages.

"Upi," he called softly, though he was already fairly certain that hers was not the voice that had called earlier, "are you all right?"

Once again there was an answering grunt, higher pitched this time, the kind of sound a female might have used to one of her young. David heard her breathe heavily as she forced herself up and stretched out her hand for him to touch. He brushed the soft fingers briefly and again withdrew his arm.

"Sleep, Upi," he whispered, satisfied.

She too sank back into the shadows, and he was about to turn away when he heard the sound of footsteps over to his right.

"Who's there?" he called out.

"Don't worry, it's only me."

He recognized Jess's voice immediately. "Where are . . . ?" he began, and stopped as she loomed up beside him—a tall, lean girl with a halo of black hair.

"I had to come," she said. "I can't stand hearing them call like that. It's awful. And I thought it might be Papio. It sounded like a male."

"Yes, but not Papio," he replied. "Probably one of the young males they brought in last week."

"But how would one of the new ones know?" she objected, thrusting her face against the mesh and peering in at the shadowy cages. "They've never been taken up there before."

3

"They seem to know just the same," he said. "Perhaps it's because they don't get fed the night before. Either that or they simply sense they're in danger."

"I guess so," she conceded. "I'm glad he's quiet now. It's horrible to think what he must be going through, all frightened and confused. . . ."

She too fell silent, listening to the small shuffling sounds that issued from the cages.

"Well," she said at last, "I'd better go. Mom's expecting me to give the twins a bath. They go nuts if anyone else tries to bathe them. You'd think I was their mother instead of their sister."

He nodded, and together they walked up to her house, further along the ridge, where they stood for a few minutes in the faint wash of light that spilled out from the broad front veranda. From within the house itself came a steady clamor of noise, voices laughing and shouting and small feet pounding along passages as Jess's five young brothers and sisters prepared for bed.

"Listen to that," Jess muttered. "It's bedlam in there."

Suddenly one of the twins' faces appeared over the edge of the veranda, her eyes mischievously wide open.

"Look at Jessica!" she shrieked. "She's outside talking to her boyfriend." She began to chant in a high teasing voice: "Jessica loves David, Jessica loves David, Jessica . . ."

"Oh, shut up!" Jess called back, yet not attempting to contradict her younger sister. To hide her embarrassment she made a mock rush at the front steps. "Go and fill the tub. I'll be in right away."

There was a scampering of feet across the veranda and again they were alone.

4

"In my next life," she said grimly, "I'm going to be an only child. Anything besides this . . ."—she waved impatiently toward the house—"this zoo! You don't realize how lucky . . ."

She stopped suddenly and bit her lip, clearly distressed by the effect her words might have on David.

"Oh hell!" she exclaimed, reaching out and gently touching his arm. "I'm sorry. I didn't mean . . . I wasn't trying . . . you know."

"It's all right," he said, his voice tight and controlled. "I don't mind so much anymore."

She gave him a look of disbelief, her hand still resting lightly on his arm.

"It must have been awful," she said sympathetically, "your mother walking out like that and taking your brother with her. The two of them going back to Australia and leaving you here with your Dad."

He turned slightly, so his expression was difficult to read in the half light.

"Not really," he answered. "Anything was better than having Mum and Dad argue all day. They just weren't getting along. It's been sort of peaceful for the past couple of months since Mum and Peter left."

Again she didn't look convinced by him. "But you must . . . well, miss them," she went on hesitantly. "I mean, people you're so close to . . . people you rely on."

He turned away even more. She could barely see his face now.

"People aren't all that matter," he said. "There are plenty of other things to take their . . ."—he quickly corrected himself—"other things to care for."

As he spoke he stared out into the darkness, in the direction of the cages. At that moment, as if some secret signal had been given, the hoarse bark was heard once more.

"Those other things," Jess said softly, responding to his unspoken thoughts, "they're not really the same. And they won't last. I'm like you, I wish they would, but they won't."

"Families don't either."

"But especially Papio and Upi," she persisted, forcing herself to go on, even though the subject was as painful to her as it was to him. "One night it will be their turn again, they'll be the ones calling. I'm sorry, David, but sooner or later they won't come back."

His reaction immediately made her regret saying that.

"No!" he said abruptly. "I won't let them take Papio and Upi again."

"But how can you stop them?" she asked reasonably.

"I'm not sure. I just know I will. Somehow." He paused, and added with an intensity that caught Jess completely off guard: "Won't you?"

She didn't answer right away, disconcerted by the question, yet unwilling to disappoint him.

"Well, won't you?" His voice was jarringly insistent.

He turned toward her then, his face calm, controlled, like a mask covering his true feelings. She tried not to look at him, wanting to make up her own mind, freely, not just to be hurried into a decision by the closed, defensive expression on his face. But again the grunting bark floated up the hillside, as if prompting her, and she found herself replying almost automatically.

6

"I'll try to stop them too," she said quietly.

"Do you really mean that?" he said with the same abrupt tone.

"Yes," she answered, curiously aware that what she was saying virtually amounted to a promise—one made not only to David but also to the animals in the silver-painted enclosure at the bottom of the slope. It was not a promise she wanted to make, she could even see how foolish it was in some ways. In that situation she simply couldn't bring herself to do otherwise. "Somehow, between us, we'll find a way," she assured him, "if we really have to."

TWO

David returned to the enclosure shortly after dawn. Walking down the hill in the clear early morning he could see that he had been right and that it was in fact one of the younger males who had called periodically through the night. The rest of the animals were undisturbed, sitting quietly in their tiny cages, idly scratching themselves or rapidly blinking their small fierce eyes as the sun rose above the ridge. Several of them called out to him as he approached, grunting or barking in a friendly way at his now familiar figure. But as always his chief concern was for Papio and Upi, who had been there in the cages when he had first arrived in Central Africa more than a year earlier.

On this, as on most mornings, Papio was the first to rise and greet him, his small pointed ears flattened against his skull, always a sure sign that he was pleased. Despite his dull coat, the result of the long period of captivity, he was a magnificent animal: a fully grown male baboon of extraordinary size, weighing over a hundred and forty pounds. Yet even more noticeable than his size was the top of his head where four shiny electrodes winked in the sunlight. These were made of some bright silvery metal that had been embedded in

his skull for experimental purposes several months earlier. Now, with the hair growing thickly around them, they were like small unnatural horns or growths. David hated the sight of them, mainly because of what they represented. Papio had once been responsive and intelligent, but since the electrodes had been implanted he had become slow and unsure of himself, apparently dull-witted.

Upi was also fully grown, though small and undersized for a mature female. She had no electrodes in her head, nor was her intelligence impaired, her bright eyes as watchful and alert as ever. But when, with a doglike bark of greeting, she rose on her hind legs, the movement cost her a visible effort and she stood quite still, panting, for several seconds. Even standing upright her body was slightly bowed, her chin and shoulders hunched forward as though trying to protect the great cross-shaped scar that disfigured her chest. This scar, like Papio's electrodes, had also been inflicted on her since David's arrival. He remembered all too well how she had once frolicked around her tiny cage, pulling excitedly at the square mesh whenever he appeared. But after her operation she had failed to recover fully, and now, months later, she could only move slowly and painfully.

David, like Jess, had found it difficult to come to terms with these disfigurements. They jolted him anew each time he saw them, and this particular morning was no exception.

"Poor Papio," he crooned as he leaned against the outer mesh and placed several slices of orange onto the dark gray flesh of the outstretched hand.

He gave the same amount to Upi, wincing slightly at

the way she grunted with the effort of leaning forward. She did not grab hungrily at the fruit as Papio had done. Instead she allowed her fingers with their gray-black nails to rest momentarily against David's, more concerned with the communion of touch than with the prospect of food.

"Eat, Upi," he said encouragingly.

But she had no appetite, as her thin shrunken haunches bore witness; and although she nipped half-heartedly at one of the pieces with her front incisors, it was done more to please him than out of hunger.

"Here, Upi," he said, "give them back."

He took the fruit from her and passed it over to Papio who quickly tore out the flesh and dutifully returned the empty rinds to David.

This returning of the rinds or any other fragment of food was a necessary part of the morning ritual. Feeding the experimental animals was strictly forbidden, and although David had long disregarded that rule, he always took care not to give himself away. He was all too aware of the possible consequences—how, once discovered, he might be officially forbidden to go near the cages again.

The feeding ritual over, he lingered beside the enclosure, whispering to the two animals, not talking sense, merely using his voice to soothe them. This too they had grown used to; it was as much a part of their daily lives as the early morning food. So that when, after only a few minutes, he began to trudge back up the hill, they both grunted out a protest at being deserted so soon.

The sun was still quite low on the horizon when he reached the house, and he expected to have at least another half hour to himself; but his father, already dressed, was waiting for him on the front veranda.

"This can't go on, David," he said quietly.

"What?" He tried to sound surprised, puzzled.

"Spending your life down there. It's becoming an obsession."

He considered taking refuge in silence, then changed his mind as he looked at his father's face.

"I don't spend my life there," he said seriously, "and it wouldn't achieve anything if I did. What they need is help, not company."

"How can anybody help them?" his father objected. "They're experimental animals. That's what they're there for—to be experimented on."

"Why not experimental humans?" he answered tersely.

His father sighed and sank back into the old Morris chair that stood near the inner wall of the veranda.

"You surely can't expect me to take that remark seriously," he said. "How on earth could you submit a human being to that treatment?"

"I couldn't. And I don't think we should submit animals to it either."

"But those baboons down there aren't just being made to suffer needlessly. Experiments carried out on them may one day save valuable human lives."

"Aren't their lives valuable too?"

"No, not in the same way. You can't measure a . . . a baboon against a human being. It doesn't make sense."

David turned and looked back down the hill, the ground now barred with yellow and black as the sun shone through the trees. He could just see a glint of silver above the grass.

"It makes sense to me," he said.

11

He heard his father jump to his feet and move impatiently away.

"For goodness' sake, David!" he burst out. "Have you lost all sense of proportion? What's got into you? You seem to care more about those animals—your blessed Papio and that other one—than you ever did about the . . . the breakup of your own family. You carry on sometimes as though they *are* your real family! As though they've taken the place of your mother and Peter!"

David turned back. His father, looking tall and nervously thin, was outlined against the vivid green and purple of the bougainvillea that grew along the side of the house.

"I don't think I understand about families," he admitted. "Not real ones. Mum was so fed up at the end that I didn't know what to do. Nor did you—you said so. And it just isn't like that with Papio. It's just . . . different somehow. Anyway, I'm sorry, Dad. About the family part, I mean. Really I am."

His father came over and put a hand on his shoulder.

"It's all right, son. Arguments like this never achieve much. In any case at fourteen you're old enough to make up your own mind about most matters, without me nagging at you. All I ask is that where those animals are concerned you don't get too involved."

"Doesn't someone have to?"

"Maybe, but not us. Bear in mind that we're guests in this country. Next year we return to Australia. In the meantime we should take care not to interfere. And that goes for Jess too."

"But Jess's ancestors came from Africa originally."

"I know, but she's still an American. Her parents, like me, are only here for one reason: to carry out research on tropical diseases. That's why our universities sent us here. It's a wonderful opportunity for all three of us. Two precious years of specialist work. And you and Jess shouldn't do anything to jeopardize that work. When we eventually go home to our own countries, it will be different. Then you'll be free to criticize the setup here as much as you like."

David walked slowly to the door.

"Jess and I don't see it that way," he said.

His father took a deep breath.

"Look," he said placatingly, "I'll tell you what I'll do. I don't normally have any contact with the animal section. But I'll go and see Ryan—he's head of animal research—and have a chat with him. It's just possible he might be able to do something about those two favorites of yours. Only possible, remember. I can't promise anything. We'll have to wait and see. But at worst you'll know where you stand. That's something, isn't it? Better than sitting around in the dark, not knowing what to expect ... I mean, how they intend ..."

His voice trailed away into awkward silence, and David, standing in the open doorway, made no effort to reply.

Later that day, in the early evening, Jess heard a Land Rover—the vehicle belonging to Mr. Anderson, David's father—drive past and stop at the garage below David's house. Less than ten minutes later, peering from her bedroom window, she saw David himself leave the house and make his way down the hill. Just from the set of his shoulders she guessed that something was wrong, and she immediately abandoned the homework she had been busy with and ran outside.

She caught up with him near the bottom of the slope, only yards from the enclosure. As they both sat down on the shadowy grass, Papio, oblivious to all but the simple fact of their presence, slapped both hands on the floor of his cage and barked out an exuberant welcome. Upi, lying on her side, rolled over and chattered loudly, making a series of short, rapid sounds that were not unlike laughter.

"Well?" Jess said quietly.

He swallowed twice, with obvious difficulty, as though something were caught in his throat.

"Ryan says that nothing can be done," he said at last.

It was the kind of news she had been dreading.

"Nothing? Why?"

He swallowed again and combed his fingers through his hair.

"He says that Upi is . . . is dying anyway."

"Oh no, not that!" Jess groaned.

"It's got something to do with a valve they put in her heart," David hurried on. "It isn't working properly. Pretty soon they'll operate again, to see what went wrong. And after that . . ."

He paused and sucked in his breath.

"But can't they mend her heart when they operate?" she asked.

"Evidently it won't be so much an operation as a . . . a sort of autopsy."

"An autopsy!" she said sharply. "You mean they won't even try and save her?"

14

He didn't answer and she looked across at the cages, to where Upi, lying carelessly stretched out on her back, was yawning lazily, revealing two rows of strong healthy teeth. To Jess, at that moment, it all seemed so grossly unfair, so stupid and wasteful.

"And Papio?" she asked, half wishing that all the rest could be left unsaid, that David could be spared the pain of going through it all again, but urged on by her growing feelings of resentment.

Again he had difficulty in answering right away.

"I'm not sure if I understand it properly," he said uncertainly. "It has to do with the electrodes. When they put them in, something happened. It could have been brain damage, or it might have been some kind of emotional reaction to the operation. A sort of withdrawal was what Dad called it. But either way, if he doesn't recover soon—the way he used to be—then he's no good to them."

"So won't they let him go?"

He shook his head dumbly.

"Dad asked about that too. Once an animal's been experimented on, it has to be . . . you know . . . put down."

"Put down!" The words burst out of her, anger completely eclipsing her former sadness. "But that's criminal! Criminal!"

"According to Ryan, it's the law . . ."

"Law!" she said, snatching the word from him. "What kind of law is that? I wonder what Ryan would think about it if he was in Papio's place? I know what I'd do with him if . . . !"

"Jess!"

She stopped abruptly, suddenly aware of the deep distress in David's eyes.

"I'm sorry," she muttered, most of her anger dissolving, leaving behind only a lingering resentment.

"Ryan says it's a way of ensuring they don't go on suffering," David explained. "A form of kindness."

"Did you say 'kindness'!"

"That's what he called it," David added lamely.

Neither of them spoke for several minutes after that. David sat bent forward, his face covered with both arms. Jess, thinking that perhaps he was crying, reached out impulsively, resting her hands gently on his back.

"Never mind," she murmured, wanting desperately to comfort him, yet not sure how to.

But when he raised his head he was dry-eyed, his face slightly altered, paler than usual and more distant.

"I'm not going to let them go," he said deliberately, his head tipped back, apparently addressing the words to the empty sky. Then to Jess, as if challenging her: "We both said we'd do something, you as well as me. It was a kind of promise, you know that. You can't go back on it now—especially not now."

She could sense that he was waiting for her response, and when she said nothing he leapt to his feet and stood facing her.

"It's no good putting it off, Jess. If we're serious about saving them, now's the time to decide."

It wasn't that she disagreed with him—simply that she was more aware of the consequences of what they might be exposing themselves to.

"It's all very well talking like that," she said defensively, "but what can we really do? The two of us?"

"Anything! It doesn't matter as long as it works."

There was a recklessness in his voice now that probed disturbingly at her own lingering sense of injustice. She twisted her hands together helplessly, not trusting herself to look either at David or at the animals squatting passively in their cages.

"You saw Upi the same as I did," he went on, "the way she looked after they brought her back here. So weak and befuddled that she couldn't . . ."

"Don't!" she broke in quickly, recoiling instinctively from the unpleasantness of the image he evoked, tears prickling unexpectedly at the back of her eyes. "You don't need to remind me of that!"

"It'll be worse next time, Jess."

"I know that too," she replied, trying to fend him off, to block out her own painful memories.

"We can't leave her then, can we?"

"But she's in a steel cage!"

"We'll cut it."

"You can't. Be practical."

"Then think of something else."

"How can we? It seems so impossible."

"We have to, Jess!"

"For a real plan, one that would work, we'd need time."

"We may not have much of that."

"Just enough to—"

"They could come for Upi tomorrow!"

He was right—she saw that clearly enough. But why, she asked herself with a last petulant show of resistance, did he have to push it all on to her? Her whole life had been like that, with her mother reminding her over and over again: You're the oldest, Jessica, the one we rely on. The oldest! The reliable one! Now here was David doing the same. It wasn't fair of him to press her so much, least of all to plead. Yet suddenly that was exactly what he was doing.

"Please, Jess, try to think of something. Please."

Acting as if he were one of her brothers or sisters; one of them always begging her, for a story, for a walk, to play some game or other. But he wasn't a child like them. Dependent. She had grown used to thinking of him as stronger than herself. More decisive. Someone to be relied on. Or was that what she had wanted to think?

"Please, Jess, please."

Openly, unashamedly appealing to her. And she knew once again that she couldn't refuse him—neither him nor the unspoken appeal of Papio and Upi watching silently from their cages.

She allowed herself to look at them now, her mind already turning to the problem of how to penetrate the enclosure. The whole structure appeared so strong and secure, seemingly impregnable. Then, as she switched her gaze to the woven mesh of the door, she noticed it. There for so long, so familiar, that she had ceased really to see it. The padlock that secured the bolt. Made not of brass or of steel; not sturdy and strong like the rest of the enclosure. Simply an old-fashioned pressed metal padlock, flimsy and cheap. Sufficient to deter the curious or to defeat the ingenuity of the cleverest baboon. But that was all.

"Wait here," she heard herself murmur.

Before she could change her mind—before the stifled voice of common sense and caution could make itself heard—she turned and ran lightly up the slope toward the garage. She was back within minutes, clutching what appeared to be a bundle of oily rags.

"Here," she said, holding the bundle out toward him.

THREE

"What is it?" David asked.

She peeled away the rags and revealed a hammer and a piece of iron rod.

"I don't see how . . ." he began.

"Here, I'll show you."

She didn't feel nearly as confident as she sounded, but she thought again of what would happen if they left the animals where they were, and some of her former anger came flooding back. Pushing David roughly aside, she thrust the iron rod through the hasp of the padlock.

"This is what we think of Ryan and his cages!" she said hotly.

She had never seen the man called Ryan, nor did she need to. At that moment he was merely a vague, threatening presence, someone who stood between her and the things she most cared for. Raising the hammer above her head, she swung it downward as hard as she could, almost as if she were striking out at the man himself.

"What are you up to?" David asked, peering over her shoulder.

By way of answer she turned and placed the remains of the padlock in his hand. Just the one blow had been enough to tear the riveted sides apart and free the hasp. The ease with which the whole thing had been accomplished sobered her slightly, making her wonder anew whether she was not simply being foolish.

David stared dully at the twisted metal, as though unsure of what he was holding. Then he began to laugh. Half turning away, he arched his body and drew back his arm.

"No!" she cried, and leapt forward, momentarily overcome by misgiving.

But she was too late. He had already flung the padlock far out into the gathering darkness. She heard it swish through the trees and land with a soft thump somewhere up the hill.

"Was that really necessary?" she said—yet realizing even as she spoke that the time for hesitation had passed. In a sense all of this had been inevitable from the moment David had appealed to her for help. No, perhaps even earlier than that: beginning on the day she had stood on this very spot, feeling outraged, and watched as Upi, still groggy from the anesthetic, had been placed back in her cage.

"What're you worrying about an old padlock for?" David said recklessly. "We won't need it again."

"Getting them out of here may not be as easy as you think," she warned him.

"What's difficult about it?" he said, laughing. "Later tonight we open the door and let them out of their cages."

"And then?"

"Why, they'll be free," he said simply. "They'll disappear."

"But where will they disappear to?" she objected.

"Apart from the town itself there's mainly farmland around here, open country for miles. Where would they hide? Upi especially, she wouldn't get far. They'd either be shot by farmers or rounded up within a few days."

She saw the grin vanish from his face.

"Are you trying to back out?" he said.

Right then and there she could think of nothing she desired more, because already she was beginning to perceive where her initial daring was leading them. But she shook her head just the same, knowing that she could never leave David to do the rest alone. The two of them were in this together, no matter where it led.

"I'm not backing out," she answered.

"So what do we do?"

Somewhere in the back of her mind an idea seemed to click into place, and suddenly it was no good trying to deny the obvious; there was only one real alternative left open to them. Yet she was unwilling to voice it aloud. It was too audacious, too extreme; and this time she wanted the suggestion to come from David; she wanted him to share the responsibility with her.

"I'm not sure," she lied.

The brief African twilight was almost over. David's face showed as a pale uncertain oval in the descending darkness.

"We'll have to get them all well away from here, won't we?" he said.

"How can we move them all? There're too many."

"Papio and Upi then," he added quickly. "We'll have to take them to some place where they'll have a chance."

"That will mean traveling miles."

She knew she sounded negative and unhelpful, but

she was still determined not to take the whole burden of decision upon herself. And David, as if sensing her predicament, immediately voiced what was in her mind.

"We'll need a car for that. One of the Land Rovers, perhaps. What do you think?"

It was not nearly as wild a suggestion as it sounded. Their parents regularly allowed them to drive along the track leading to the public road; and although they were far from expert, they were both reasonably competent.

"You do realize what terrible trouble we'll get into?" she cautioned him.

"I've already told you, I don't care what we do as long as it works. We can worry about everything else afterward."

"The police will probably be called in," she persisted, testing her own resolve as much as David's. "Technically, it will be stealing."

"And what will it be if we leave them here, if we let Ryan have his way? Isn't there a technical word for that too?"

It was the one argument calculated to still all her doubts, and almost with a sense of relief, she relented.

———————————

As arranged, they met soon after midnight. By then there was a sliver of moon quite high in the sky, and Jess, creeping quietly down the hill, could just make out David's figure standing beside the enclosure. They had both brought knapsacks with them, slung over their shoulders, but whereas Jess's contained only a few essential items, David's was packed full of gear.

"You look as though you're set for a long-distance hike," she whispered.

He laughed softly.

"No harm in being prepared, especially as we plan to get well off the main road. If anything goes wrong we may have to walk out, perhaps even spend a night in the bush."

"And the car keys?"

He jingled them in the darkness.

Together they opened the door of the enclosure and crept inside. Although it was open to the sky it smelled strongly of cheap disinfectant. One of the males near the back, alarmed by the intrusion, let out a loud bark that disturbed several of the other animals, but they soon settled down.

Working quickly and silently, Jess slipped the catch on Upi's cage and eased open the wire door. They were both prepared to lift her out, but she seemed to understand what was happening. With a single surprisingly agile movement she swung herself through the opening and down onto the concrete floor. Her breathing, although hoarse and heavy, was reassuringly even.

"Good girl," Jess whispered, stroking her head.

She chittered lightly in response. Now that she was outside her cage she crouched nervously, close to their legs.

Getting Papio out proved more difficult. The activity and the whispering had bewildered him, and he clung to the wire at the back of the cage. Watching him, the way he drew back his lips in a nervous grin, revealing long, vicious canines, Jess fleetingly wondered whether they were being foolish. Papio was powerful enough to kill either of them with a single lunge.

"Do you think he's safe?" she said uncertainly.

But David only laughed.

"Don't be silly."

To prove his point, he reached into the cage and stroked the side of Papio's muzzle.

"Come on, my beautiful," he crooned, "come on now."

The gentle caress and the soothing words were all that were needed. Releasing his hold on the wire, Papio shuffled across the metal floor and dropped down beside them.

"Stage one complete," David said, as though checking items on an agenda.

He turned toward the door and was about to leave when Jess drew him back.

"Shouldn't we put our belts around their necks . . . or something . . . ?"

As with her previous suggestion, he dismissed it carelessly.

"Don't worry. They won't go rushing off without us. You'll see."

Once again he was proved right. When they left the enclosure and made their way diagonally across the hillside to the dark outline of the garage, the two animals followed their every move—walking on all fours close beside them or sitting quietly on the grass.

To begin with, they paused every few paces so Upi could rest; but it soon became apparent that although she was short of breath she was capable of walking slowly for a sustained period. She even managed to scramble up into the back of the Land Rover unaided. This time Papio followed her example without hesitation.

"So far, so good," David whispered, sliding into the driver's seat. "Now for the difficult part."

"You said it," Jess murmured apprehensively, climbing in beside him.

Yet to their amazement it all proved surprisingly easy. The engine started on the first try, and without any grating of gears or stalling, the Land Rover rolled out of the garage and along the track that led up and over the ridge. To their right, the two houses showed as blurred humps against the night sky. Jess watched them anxiously, but no lights appeared in the windows, no shouts of alarm were heard in the darkness. Within minutes they were clear, whirring over the cattle grid and out onto the public road.

Skirting the town was just as straightforward. At that time of the morning they encountered hardly any traffic, and almost before they realized their good fortune they had left the lighted area behind and were traveling along the main route south.

"I think we've done it!" David said excitedly. "D'you realize that? We've got them away from that rotten place forever!"

He bounced up and down on the seat, releasing some of the pent-up tension of the past few hours. Papio and Upi, thinking he was inviting them to play, crept forward and patted his shoulders tentatively.

"You see," he said delightedly, "they understand."

But Jess, glancing over her shoulder, saw only two frightened and bewildered animals.

After that they settled down to the long journey ahead: David, intent on driving, yet conscious of Papio's warm muzzle against his cheek; Jess with her arm held protectively around Upi, who had climbed into the front seat between them.

Soon they were passing through the small town of Chingwe. They both looked nervously at the glowing blue lamp outside the police station and were glad to leave it behind. Rattling now over the steel bridge that crossed the Chingwe river—the river itself, with its swirling current and its broad banks of reed, gleaming in the faint moonlight. Then abandoning the main highway that led through flat bush or farmland to Livingstone and the Victoria Falls, and taking instead the shorter, steeper road that climbed up over the escarpment and down to the tiny settlement of Modanda on the banks of the Zambezi.

Again everything seemed to go smoothly. The Land Rover negotiated the foothills with ease and later wound steadily up toward the heights that stood above the huge Zambezi valley. But just as they were nearing the top of the range their luck ran out, and they drove into a heavy belt of early morning mist. It lay between the folds of the hills like a soft, smothering blanket, so thick in places that they could barely see the broken line in the middle of the road.

Now it was all they could do to keep moving. At a snail's pace they topped the highest point and began the long descent. Originally they had hoped to find tire tracks that would lead them deep into the bush somewhere along the lower edge of the escarpment. But, with the mist obliterating the sides of the road, that was out of the question. They were only free to follow the narrow strip of tarmac deeper and deeper into the valley. And as the miles ticked slowly by, a new worry presented itself. Traveling blind in the mist, they had lost all sense of distance; for all they knew, the riverside settlement of Modanda could have been around the very next bend. And with its hotel and police station and customs post, it was the last place they wanted to stumble on.

"It's no good," David said anxiously, "we can't go on like this. We seem to have been traveling downhill for ages."

Jess nodded. "If it would only clear for a minute or two. It's too late to look for tracks, but if we could just find somewhere to pull off the road, anything, as long as . . ."

She paused as a breath of wind stirred the mist, lifting it clear of them for a few brief seconds.

"There!" she cried, pointing to the left—to a narrow space between gnarled shapes of trees.

David swung the wheel and nosed the Land Rover through the gap just as the whiteness closed around them. They bumped across a shallow ditch, labored a few yards up a steep incline, and found their way totally blocked by a huge baobab tree—its smooth gray trunk, more than ten feet across, rising straight out of a tangle of roots that extended for another ten feet on either side. There was no going beyond such an obstacle, and reluctantly David turned off the ignition. As the engine died, the stillness of the surrounding bush crept in on them: an almost deathly quiet, with even the insects silenced by the oppressive blanket of mist.

"End of the line," David said evenly.

All at once he both appeared and acted unduly tired, lying sprawled back in his seat with his eyes closed, as though the whole trip had been too much for him. By contrast the two animals, after hours of fitful dozing, had perked up and were staring about them, Upi with obvious curiosity and Papio with his habitually puzzled expression.

"Time for the grand farewell," Jess said, trying to ease David over the pain of parting by making a joke of it.

She opened the door and climbed out, urging Upi to follow. David didn't move.

"Come on," she said encouragingly.

"In a minute."

"Putting it off will only make it worse." She was coaxing him now, employing the same tone of voice she used on her young brothers and sisters.

He dragged both hands down his face in a weary gesture that made Jess want to reach out and touch him reassuringly.

"It's just that I'm so tired," he complained.

"I know," she murmured, "but there'll be plenty of time to sleep once they've gone."

"If I could doze for a few minutes, that's all," he pleaded with her, so that Jess had to force herself to refuse.

"Yes, but later. It's their time we're wasting now."

That seemed to rouse him slightly. He rubbed his hand across his eyes in an oddly dazed way and shook his head, as though trying to clear it.

"Yes . . . their time . . . theirs . . ."

He shook his head again, looking so lonely and forlorn that Jess was on the point of telling him that it didn't matter, he could leave it all to her if that made him feel better. But while she was still searching for the right words, he seemed to explode into action. Sliding quickly across the seat, he leapt out on Jess's side, dragging Papio after him. Before she could stop him or protest he had herded the two animals together and pushed them forcibly away.

"Go on!" he said roughly. "Get away from here! Clear out!"

With the heavy mist swirling about them, they shambled uncertainly into the bright beams of the headlights, clinging to each other in their bewilderment.

"Didn't you hear me? We don't want you here! Shove off!"

They didn't move, remaining in a crouched, defensive position, their small eyes dazzled by the brightness.

"Give them a chance . . ." Jess pleaded.

"This is their chance!" he interrupted her, his voice far too loud in the stillness of the early morning. "They have to take it while they can. Go on! Run! Like this!"

He began to climb over the twisted roots of the baobab, heading up the slope; and the animals, after a moment's indecision, followed him. When they were about twenty feet away he left them and scrambled back down to where Jess was standing. Vaguely, through the mist, at the very limit of the glow cast by the headlights, they could make out the hazy outline of two furry shapes. Neither animal moved. They were sitting up beside a wind-scarred outcrop of rock, staring down at the twin eyes of light.

"We'll have to be patient," Jess murmured. "It's all strange to them."

The seconds lengthened into minutes and still nothing happened. Then, very slowly, Papio dropped onto all fours and began to descend the slope, the tiny electrodes buried deep in his skull shining brightly as he drew closer.

"Shoo!" Jess shouted, waving her arms wildly. "Scat!"

But Papio ignored her, continuing to descend, with Upi only a foot or two behind.

"Go away," she almost pleaded.

And still they advanced, past the dazzling lights to where Jess and David waited helplessly.

"You see!" David cried. "They won't leave us! They won't!"

There was in his voice, Jess noticed uneasily, a distinct ring of triumph, as though this were, after all, exactly what he had hoped for.

FOUR

At Jess's insistence they spent the next hour or more trying to encourage the animals to head off into the bush, but their efforts proved hopelessly inadequate. Neither Papio nor Upi showed any desire for freedom. The surrounding bush, with its strange shapes and smells, obviously daunted them. They clearly preferred the security of human company—so much so that all Jess's shouting and shooing and stamping of feet produced nothing more than amazed stares or a feeble puzzled bark. And the moment she paused for breath, Upi came sidling up and pushed her warm muzzle into her hand, as if to say, "Don't worry, we're still here."

"It's no use," Jess said, throwing her arms up helplessly, "we're not getting anywhere."

Dawn had broken by then, the daylight filtering down through the mist that, although less dense, still clung to the hillside. In the uncertain light Jess and David looked exhausted: their eyes red-rimmed, their faces drawn, their clothes saturated by the moisture-laden air.

"If you ask me," Jess went on, "we're the ones who should clear out. Just drive off and let them fend for themselves."

But David, who had done little to help her since his initial efforts, shook his head. He was sitting on the hood of the Land Rover, his wet hair plastered to his forehead.

"We can't leave them here," he said. "They might wander into the road and get caught again—or worse. In any case it's too late to talk of driving off. We've had the lights on all this time and the battery must be flat as a pancake. You'll never get this heap moving again."

"Are you sure?"

"Check for yourself."

She ran around to the driver's side and switched on the ignition key, but all she heard was a faint click.

"Dead as a doornail."

She climbed out and stood staring in moody silence at the two animals. Papio, completely unaware of the trouble he was causing, leapt lightly up beside David. He was wet from the mist and dew, with countless tiny droplets clinging to his rich grayish-brown fur. Giving his whole body a vigorous shake, he sent a shower of water in all directions.

"Watch what you're doing," David said, grinning and shoving playfully at the powerful shoulders.

Papio immediately joined in what he considered a desirable game, pawing gently at David's face. Even Upi tried to take part, ambling forward and clambering slowly up onto the hood.

"Oh, for God's sake!" Jess said with disgust. "This isn't the time for playing!"

Shooing them away from the Land Rover, she again set about trying to chase them off. This time she didn't waste energy waving her arms around and shouting. Instead she picked up a stone and threw it so that it just missed them, the stone itself bouncing off a rock and landing at Papio's feet. Instantly, Upi made a frightened yakking noise and began to sidle away. Papio, more slow-witted and simply puzzled by her behavior, held his ground. Swinging his head quizzically from side to side, he looked from her to the stone and back again, repeating that action several times. Then, finally solving the problem to his own satisfaction, he picked up the stone and brought it over to her.

"I told you," David said, a knowing smile on his face, "you won't make them go."

"I will if I hurt them," Jess replied quickly, "if I actually hit them with the stones."

But it was an empty threat that she could never have carried through, as David was fully aware.

"You wouldn't do that," he said quietly.

"All right," she countered, "what can you suggest?"

He shrugged, gazing thoughtfully up in the direction of the escarpment. Already the mist was beginning to dissolve, revealing wooded slopes and the ghostly shapes of trees. Immediately above them the craggy branches of the baobab sprouted from the massive trunk like spiky tentacles.

"There's only one thing for it," he said, "we'll have to walk them out of here. Take them up into the thick forest where no one will find them."

She was given little time to ponder his suggestion. A light breeze had sprung up, tearing what remained of the mist into thin isolated patches, allowing the sunlight to break through and flood the whole valley. And there, not far below them, clearly visible above the tops of the trees, was the settlement of Modanda. Its cluster of red roofs glowed richly in the morning sunlight, and just beyond could be seen the glittering sweep of the suspension bridge that crossed the river.

"Let's get the hell out of here!" David said urgently. "The first car to go past will spot the Land Rover, and before you know it the place will be swarming with cops."

He had already shouldered his bag and was urging the two baboons up the rocky slope in a northerly direction, clearly intending to head for the cover of the heavily wooded hillsides.

"Aren't you coming?" he asked, glancing around.

Jess was still standing beside the Land Rover.

"I'm not sure it's such a good idea to go with them," she said.

"Why not?"

"Because . . . because it's hard enough leaving them now," she explained hesitantly, groping for a means of expressing not so much her personal fears as her fears for David. "The longer we stay with them . . ."

"You're not going to let us down now, are you?" he broke in, sounding hurt and disappointed.

He had turned and was gazing straight at her, the same lonely, forlorn expression on his face that she had noticed earlier.

"It's not a case of letting you down," she began, trying to reason with him, "it's more . . ."

But the expression on his face didn't change, and with a sigh she also shouldered her knapsack.

"Okay. Let's go. But not up there."

All at once, relieved of the frustration of the past hour or more, she felt calm and cool-headed, confident of what now had to be done.

"I think this way would be safer," she added, pointing downhill, toward the southeast.

"But that's the wrong direction."

"It's like you said, the police will be after us before long. The first place they'll look will be up there, and it'll be no good trying to make a run for it with Upi. What we have to do is throw them off the scent. I'll show you what I mean."

It took them barely ten minutes to reach the Zambezi. The great river, several hundred yards wide, swirled past at their feet, straining at the banks of coarse reed that lined either shore. Now, with the rainy season well advanced, the current was running strong and deep, especially out in the center where logs and islands of reeds were being carried along.

"We can't cross that," David said, "not unless we use the bridge."

But Jess was already pointing downstream, to a flat expanse of rock that formed a long narrow bluff just above the level of the river.

"It follows the river for at least a mile," she said. "I remembered it from a camping trip we made here once."

"I see what you're getting at. While we're on the rock we won't leave a trail for people to follow."

Nor was that the only advantage of Jess's plan. It also enabled them to put a respectable distance between themselves and any possible pursuer without seriously taxing Upi. On the flat, even surface she was perfectly able to keep up a steady walking pace—her breathing always rasping and loud, yet never distressed.

By mid-morning they were miles downstream. They stopped briefly, in the shade of a large fever tree, and ate some of the sandwiches they had brought, sharing the food out between themselves and the two animals. To their delight, Upi showed a real appetite for the first time in weeks, eagerly snatching up whatever was tossed to her and barking out a protest when no more was forthcoming.

"Hush!" David cautioned her, glancing nervously back over the way they had come.

There was only one person in sight—a lone African fisherman, about half a mile upstream, paddling his dugout along the very edge of the reed bank where the current was at its weakest. It was unlikely that he had seen them or heard Upi above the rushing murmur of the river in flood. But there was nothing to be gained by taking chances, and David and Jess rose wearily to their feet.

As agreed, they turned away from the river at this point and headed north, following a rocky watercourse that snaked its way up into the hills. Within an hour they were into thickly wooded country. Now they had to travel far more slowly, allowing Upi to set her own pace over the boulder-strewn streambed. More and more frequently as the day wore on, she was forced to rest, lying sprawled out on the cool sand, panting heavily. Jess and David watched her anxiously, and Papio, obviously puzzled by her behavior, hovered over her, sometimes gently grooming her where she lay. But always she recovered quickly and was soon toiling steadily on.

On several occasions they startled animals that had come down to the watercourse to drink from the murky pools. Usually these were buck that leapt noisily away through the undergrowth; but once they came upon a large female warthog and her twin young. She stared aggressively past the two baboons at the human intruders, her tail up, her massive head half lowered as though she were about to charge—and this time it was Jess and David who had to retreat, back down the valley until she had trotted off.

That encounter, more even than the steady passage of time, brought home to Jess the hazardous nature of their position, and she stopped where she was, on a narrow stretch of river sand, leaving David to walk on alone.

"We should be heading back soon," she called after him. "We'd be idiots to get caught up here in the dark."

He mumbled something in reply, not bothering to turn around.

"David," she called out more sharply, "we can't go on climbing up here forever. Isn't this far enough?"

"Just about," he said vaguely, still not turning to her. A little further . . . another half hour or so . . ."

"All right," she conceded, falling into her usual habit of soothing him, "another half hour, but that's all."

She hurried to catch up with him, feeling hot and sticky despite the overhang of trees that shaded the watercourse. She had expected the temperature to fall as they climbed, but now the air actually felt hotter, the atmosphere dense and still, almost oppressive. Ahead of them, Upi, suffering as much from the heat as from exhaustion, had stopped yet again. She lay on her side, her chest working rhythmically and fast as she took short gasping breaths. Jess went to her and stroked her side while David collected water in his cupped hands from one of the brackish pools. Stooping over her, he allowed a little of it to dribble between her open jaws. She lapped at it, her eyes half closed.

"There," he said lovingly, "there. You'll be fine in a minute."

They crouched beside her, waiting for her breathing to return to normal. All around them the forest had grown strangely quiet; even the persistent whistle of cicadas was subdued and distant. Somewhere over to their right a bird called—a cool, clear sound piercing the heavy atmosphere of the afternoon. The same call rang out a second and a third time, and suddenly Jess leapt to her feet.

"That bird!" she said quickly. "It's a hoopoe! A rain bird!"

She looked up at the line of the forest high above them. Heavy black clouds were massed across the sky. They seemed to be boiling over the edge of the escarpment, obliterating the heights, tumbling into the valley. A blast of cold, moist wind swept down the gully in which they stood, and to a distant accompaniment of thunder, the sun disappeared.

It was too late now to think of retreat; she knew that would have to wait. On every side she could hear the crisp smack of raindrops striking leaves, the isolated sounds growing into a steady murmur.

"We have to get out of this gully," she said urgently. "There could be a flood down here any minute."

David nodded and stood up.

"That's just what we need," he said cheerfully. "It'll wipe out any tracks we've left. They'll never find us then."

"You mean they'll never find Upi and Papio," Jess corrected him.

"Same thing," he replied, and laughed.

Jess did not bother to argue with him—not then. The rain was growing heavier, some of the larger drops breaking through the canopy and splashing down onto her bare skin. She shivered slightly. Something warm and soft touched her hand and she looked down into Papio's puzzled eyes. He could obviously sense danger, but he was merely bewildered by it, as he was by so much that had happened recently. He made a small, nervous yakking noise, appealing to Jess who stroked his head and then turned to the exhausted female.

"Come on, girl," she said encouragingly.

Upi, partially recovered, rose slowly onto all fours. In contrast to Papio, she took in the situation with a few swift glances. Then, without needing to be directed, she led the way up the bank and into the cover of the forest. There, on suitably high ground, they took refuge under the biggest tree they could find, the four of them crouched closely together. David had taken a plastic raincoat from his knapsack, and with this covering them they were reasonably well protected.

That was just as well because soon afterward the storm struck in earnest. Squall after squall of rain lashed the hillside, the thunder shaking the ground beneath their feet and causing the baboons to grunt with alarm. Somewhere in the distance another more ominous sound made itself heard. Faint to begin with, it grew into a dull roar, and suddenly the first wave of the flood came tearing down the gully, heaving between the earth banks and tumbling branches and boulders that lay in its path.

The noise of rain and flood, interspersed with thunder, was deafening, a steady, strident clamor that seemed to assault the senses. And Jess, leaning back against the tree, closed her eyes and buried her head in her arms, wishing she could spirit herself away, back home to the warmth and comfort of her own room.

It wasn't her intention to doze off—she only wanted to escape the discomfort and the awful noise—but very gradually the general din receded from her, drifting off until it was little more than a background murmur. Finally it disappeared altogether, giving way to a warm, dark place as, slowly, she fell into a deep sleep of exhaustion.

When she awoke it was late afternoon, the sun striking slantwise through the trees. David was sitting on the bank of the gully, tossing sticks into the small stream, which was all that remained of the flood. There was no sign of either of the animals. Jess pushed aside the raincoat and sat up.

"Have they gone?" she asked.

David glanced over his shoulder.

"Feel better?"

"Where are they?"

"What? Oh, them. They're busy feeding . . . greenery and insects and stuff . . . anything they can find. Been at it for a couple of hours."

"You mean they've gone?"

"Oh no, they're somewhere around. All we have to do is call them."

He put both hands to his mouth, in order to demonstrate.

"No, don't!" Jess said. "This is the chance we need. If we creep off now they won't catch us before dark. And without our company to lure them away, they'll probably stay here."

She was already folding the raincoat, stuffing it into the bag.

"I don't think we should leave them just yet," David said.

"Why not? This is the perfect opportunity."

His back was toward her, his head turned slightly as he stared up at the line of the escarpment, which was tinged with yellow by the late afternoon sunlight.

"It will be night soon," he said. "We'll never find our way out in the dark."

"Of course we will. We both have flashlights. All we need to do is follow the gully as far as the river, then walk upstream until we reach the bridge."

"It's risky," he murmured.

"Risky?" she said incredulously. "Just think about what's happened so far: We've stolen two experimental animals, not to mention a Land Rover, driven without a license, purposely avoided any search parties, and finally survived a flood. After all that, what's the big deal about walking home?"

He didn't answer, his back stiff and straight.

"Well?"

"I'm still not leaving them," he said decisively.

Jess experienced a sudden sinking feeling in the pit of her stomach, all her previous unacknowledged fears focused on this moment.

"But we have to," she reasoned with him. "They belong here and we don't."

He turned toward her, his face streaked with shadow.

"I belong here too, for the time being."

"What do you mean, for the time being? How long is that?"

"Until they're safe."

She went over and knelt in front of him, her face only a foot from his, looking into his eyes.

"Don't you understand?" she said patiently. "They'll never be safe. There's no safety for wild animals. For these two especially. Papio can't think straight anymore, and Upi's as weak as a kitten. I'm sorry about that, the same as you, but that's the way it is. They have to take their chances. I thought we both realized that before we started out."

"Until they're safe . . ." he repeated mechanically, his eyes flickering past her face, refusing to acknowledge her.

"You'll have to do better than that, David."

He hesitated.

"I can't . . ." he added uncertainly, "not yet . . . while they're here with us . . . wanting . . . together, all of us . . . wanting . . ."

Jess was never quite sure what it was that fully alerted her—his tone of voice perhaps, because the words themselves were hardly more than a jumble—but all at once she realized what had begun to happen.

"They're not human beings, David!" she burst out.

"They're animals! It's not fair to them to try and make them into something they're not. They can never . . ."

She stopped as he flinched away. For a second she thought he was going to answer her; but instead he closed his eyes and mouth together, in an act of total rejection, as though he were willing her to disappear.

"All right," she said in a sudden burst of annoyance, "if that's the way you want it, I won't interfere!"

She was too angry now to think clearly, reacting much as she had on the previous evening, when David had told her about Ryan, her sense of outrage and frustration completely clouding her reason.

"I'm leaving here right now," she rasped out, "and you can come or stay as you like."

She leapt to her feet and marched resolutely downhill, weaving an erratic path between the trees and bushes.

"They're all the same!" she muttered through clenched teeth. "They just want to use the animals! That's all! David too. As bad as Ryan . . . as bad . . ."

But even in her present state of mind she could not sustain that comparison; and as she recognized the absurdity of linking Ryan and David, of even mentioning them in the same breath, her anger left her.

Almost guiltily, she glanced back up the hillside, feeling now not merely foolish but ashamed.

"David?" she called out in a worried voice. "David!"

And when he didn't answer, she ran back over the way she had come.

He was exactly as she had left him, sitting on the bank, his eyes and mouth firmly closed, but he must have heard her because as she approached he became visibly less tense. He was still as obstinately cut off from her as before, yet now his face appeared more sad than determined. Just for an instant he looked almost as lost and bewildered as Papio—Papio, locked in his cage, gazing out onto a world he had ceased to comprehend. It was only a momentary impression, but Jess, unable to prevent herself, reached out and pulled him toward her. He resisted at first, and then gave in completely, pushing his face into the hollow of her neck and nestling against her, as though trying to escape from the present into a past he had somehow lost.

Up until that moment she had always regarded David as a close friend, as someone of her own age whom she liked and . . . There was, she knew, much more to it than that, something understood by both of them, which they had not needed to speak about. But now all that was gone. No, not just gone—different. With her arms about him he felt so much younger, a child almost, and she correspondingly so much older. Old enough to . . . She stopped herself from thinking that, yet the gulf remained, bridged only by care; by her own cradling arms, the way she held him now, protectively, rocking him gently to and fro.

"A little longer then," she murmured, sadly aware that she was incapable of walking back down the hillside a second time, of leaving him alone with the night approaching, "until they're both safe."

FIVE

Jess awoke in the early hours, just as the night was growing chill. The fire was almost out, and she crept forward and fed it with small pieces of wood. Like everything else, the wood was damp from the recent storm, giving off more smoke than flame, but any kind of fire was better than nothing, and the smoke did help keep the mosquitoes away.

No longer sleepy, she sat close to the warmth, listening to the ceaseless clamor of insect noise. She still felt a little panicky at finding herself in such a situation—though she was aware that they could have been much worse off. If David had not had the foresight to bring matches, there would not even have been this fire. Nor was that all. Among the many things crammed into his knapsack were a knife, another flashlight with an extra supply of batteries, and what she had mistaken at first for a bundle of dry sticks.

"Take a second look," he had said, laughing. "It's dried meat, what people here call biltong. It won't go bad in the heat, so it's perfect for a trip like this."

It was good to know they had a basic supply of food. Yet equally she had been slightly disturbed to learn that his choosing to stay out there in the bush had not been a spur of the moment impulse. He must have planned it all from the start, carefully selecting those few essential items they needed to survive. In a sense he had tricked her. And worse than that, he had demonstrated how little she really knew him. Behind the close friend there had lurked a stranger.

She looked across at him now, his face peaceful and untroubled as he slept. He seemed so known, so familiar. And yet . . .

She hunched closer to the fire, feeding it with more of the half-dry pieces of wood. Somewhere on the cliffs high above them a baboon barked, the sound carrying sharp and clear through the background murmur of insect noise. David stirred restlessly and opened his eyes. For a few seconds he gazed at her blankly; and then, fully awake, he sat up and stared wildly about him.

"Where are they?" he asked anxiously.

"Don't worry, they haven't gone."

"Yes, but where . . . ?"

"They weren't happy here by the fire. It frightened them. After you fell asleep they climbed up into the trees. They've been quiet ever since."

She reached for the flashlight and shone it upward. Both animals were perched about thirty feet from the ground, crouched securely within the forks of branches. They blinked sleepily in the light.

"Just like babes in the wood," David commented, obviously satisfied.

"Who? Them or us?"

He smiled and moved closer to the fire.

"I suppose us, if we're going to be honest," he admitted. "After all, this is home for them. We're the ones who've wandered from the family hearth."

His frankness and his easy manner belied completely his earlier behavior, and Jess, encouraged by the change in him, said quietly:

"Speaking of families, don't you think we should find some way of letting ours know we're safe?"

He seemed to consider the suggestion seriously.

"No, not yet. I'd rather do what we came here for first—you know, get Papio and Upi settled. Make sure they can fend for themselves."

"Is that what you want?"

"What I want . . . ?"

"For them to be really independent of us."

"Yes, of course."

"And for us to leave them once they can stand on their own feet?"

He was sitting close beside her, and she turned and watched him carefully, waiting for his reaction. But he merely nodded and continued to gaze into the flames.

"I thought that was the whole point," he said easily.

"What you said . . . the way you acted earlier . . . ?" she began tentatively.

"Oh that," he said and tossed a fragment of kindling carelessly into the flames, "that was nothing. Just me carrying on like a kid. I must have been a bit overtired. I get like that sometimes."

He spoke so naturally, so without reserve or embarrassment, that Jess could hardly suppress a sigh of relief. It was like rediscovering the real David, the person she had known, after being convinced that she had lost him. And, in spite of everything that had happened, she felt relaxed and happy—even pleasantly tired. She leaned against him, her eyes closed, allowing herself to drift off into sleep. But while she was still only dozing, a wild baboon somewhere high above them again broke the silence with a short fierce bark. David's whole body immediately stiffened and she drew quickly away from him. He was gazing intently up into the darkness, his hands already curled around his mouth. Taking a deep breath, he let out a low snorting reply that was very nearly indistinguishable from the original bark.

Delighted with the result, he turned eagerly toward her, as though seeking her approval.

"Not bad for a first try, was it?" he said. "Give me a chance to get some practice and I'll improve a lot. Anyone listening will think it's another baboon. The real thing. It'll be impossible to tell the difference in the end."

He cupped his hands and repeated the sound: the same fierce animal cry, yet this time so authentic that it totally shattered Jess's newly acquired peace of mind.

"How about that?" he said proudly.

She didn't answer. But long after he had curled up beside the fire and fallen asleep, his head resting peacefully on her lap, she continued wide awake, staring into the uncertain, shifting pattern of the flames.

The worst heat of the day was over, and Jess, leaving the deep shade in which they had spent the past few hours, walked up the gully to the flat, more exposed area of rock. From there she turned and faced back down the valley, waiting for the cool breeze that wafted up from the river in the late afternoon.

After nearly three days in the bush she felt grubby and uncomfortable. Her clothes were crumpled and smeared with dirt, her skin sticky with stale sweat, her hair a hopeless tangle in which tiny fragments of leaf and dry twig were lodged. She was fingering it distastefully when the first snatch of breeze brushed her cheek, and gratefully she closed her eyes, enjoying the cool touch.

At the first sign of a breeze David also left the shade and walked up toward her.

"What are you acting so dreamy about?" he asked.

Despite his dirty and disheveled appearance he was cheerful and relaxed.

"I'm trying to imagine myself in a deep, cool bath," she said. "One of those bubbly ones you see in movies."

"Why waste your time thinking about baths? Look at those two down there. Never been washed in their lives—and as sleek and healthy as you please."

"Yes, but they're protected by fur," she retorted.

He reached out playfully and brushed his hand against her untidy mop of hair.

"Speaking of fur, you're not doing too badly yourself."

She grinned, pushing his hand away.

"And what about you? You're not exactly a hairdresser's advertisement."

"Me? Haven't you noticed? Fur sprouting out all over the place. The result of not bathing. The body returns naturally to its primeval state."

Laughing to himself, he continued up the gully to a point where he had a clear view of the cliff that fronted the top edge of the escarpment. There he stopped and tried out some of the new baboon sounds he had acquired. Only that morning he had managed to get a response from a troop of wild baboons. No reply came from them now, but he went on practicing just the same.

To Jess the whole performance was vaguely disquieting, and she consciously tried to shut it out, concentrating all her attention on Papio and Upi.

They had spent most of the afternoon dozing or quietly grooming each other—gently parting their fur and searching for fleas or ticks or small crystals of salt. Now they too emerged from the shade, Upi leading the way across the gully and up onto a previously unexplored bank. While she nipped at fresh shoots, Papio turned over logs and small stones, looking for beetles and grubs and anything else remotely edible.

They were soon engrossed in their simple activities, and Jess, watching from above, was amazed afresh at the ease with which they had adapted to their new lifestyle. Apart from Papio's dependence on David, which was as strong as ever, they were completely at home here, acting exactly like animals that had spent all their lives in the bush.

Perhaps it was the sense that she was observing two essentially wild creatures that affected Jess so forcibly, because suddenly she had the feeling that she was a total outsider. Someone who didn't belong. An alien looking in on a world she could have no share of. And somehow—though she didn't quite know why—David's incessant imitations droning on in the background only served to intensify that feeling. He was a part of that closed inner world too. She was the only one excluded.

"Upi," she called, instinctively wanting to establish contact, "come here, girl, come."

Upi raised her eyes and gazed at her. It was a keen, questioning look, intelligent, trusting, and for a moment Jess felt less set apart. Then something about the quality of the afternoon seemed to change. It took her a while to realize what it was—the silence, the fact that David was no longer calling up toward the distant cliffs.

She glanced around and saw that he had disappeared from view. In that same instant Papio gave a troubled bark and loped past her, his small eyes searching the banks on either side of the gully. Upi, moving more slowly and carefully, followed him, so that now Jess was truly alone. Sitting on a rock in the middle of nowhere with only the drowsy whir of insects to keep her company.

She knew where they had gone—and that Papio was never at ease unless he had David in sight—but she made herself remain still. Let them go, she thought. Why should she mind if they left her? Wasn't this what she had wanted—to break the lines that held them to her? David, after all, had to make his own choices; she couldn't hover over him or them indefinitely. Eventually . . . even if it meant . . . she would have . . .

Gradually the stillness of the afternoon crept in on her—that and her usual protective concern for David weakening her resolve. She rose involuntarily to her feet.

"David!"

There was no answer—only the pale blue sky with its flat-bottomed summer clouds pressing down from above, the tall, feathery grasses standing like two enclosing walls on either bank. Turning, she made her way rapidly up the gully.

She quickly found them. All three were crouched together; David bent over while the animals gently groomed him, their dark fingers searching through his hair.

"What the hell do you think you're doing!" she burst out.

He looked at her and smiled.

"You could call it fraternizing with the natives."

"What's that supposed to mean?"

"The local barbershop, then, does that satisfy you?"

She went over and pulled him forcibly away from the two animals.

"What's your problem, Jess? " he asked, standing up and facing her. "They were only being friendly."

"Is that all it was? Being friendly?"

"All right, let's give it its proper name. They were delousing me. After three days in the bush, sleeping out, you could do with some of that yourself."

"You're just making excuses. You were encouraging them, you know you were."

"To do what?"

"To think of you as a baboon."

"They don't need any encouragement. Hasn't it occurred to you? As far as they're concerned we're two almost hairless versions of themselves. That's how they see us."

"And how do we see ourselves, David?"—her voice level and controlled.

He shrugged.

"I don't think that's a very important question at this stage," he said indifferently.

"So what *do* you consider important?"

He too grew abruptly serious. Waving his hand at the surrounding bush, he said:

"Managing to survive, here, in this. That's all that matters for the moment. We're the learners here, Jess. And I don't care how we see ourselves, or even what we are, as long as it helps us stay alive."

She had to admit that in a way he was right. Survival was a real issue. That fact became steadily clearer as the days went by.

For one thing, those slopes and ridges weren't merely a haven for Jess and her companions but for a host of other creatures, many of them dangerous—such as the wild pig and elephant that fed on the rich growth along the edges of the gullies.

Yet it was not only animals that threatened them. There was also the climate to contend with. After that first wild storm, no other rain had fallen. Every afternoon dark clouds built up on the horizon, but they always circled around and drifted away. So that by the morning of the sixth day the gully was dry except for a few pools filled as much with mud as with water. This did not seem to bother the baboons at all. They lapped happily at the murky surface just as though it were a clear running stream. When Jess and David tried to copy them, they were left with a mouthful of gritty sludge in which live mosquito larvae twisted and squirmed. Jess spat it out in disgust and wiped her mouth with the back of her hand.

"It's no good," she said, "we'll have to go back down to the river."

"We can't drag Upi all that way just for our sakes," David objected. "It wouldn't be fair."

"Then what do we do?"

"We could try filtering what we have."

Taking off his shirt, he fashioned it into a crude form of bag, filled it with some of the sludge, and then sucked the moisture through the cloth. Surprisingly it worked: The water tasted unpleasantly warm and musty, but it was comparatively free of sand and other debris.

"What about this then?" David said, his face streaked with dirty water. "A shower and a drink all in one!"

She smiled half heartedly.

"We can't go on like this, David."

He looked at her, surprised.

"Why not?"

"Because these pools will be even lower tomorrow."

"There may be rain before then," he said optimistically. "It's too early for the rainy season to be over. We must get a storm soon."

"Even supposing we do, there's still the question of food. Hardly any of the biltong's left. What happens when that's gone?"

"We improvise," he replied. "Like I said, we're the learners here."

As good as his word, he tried that afternoon to eat the tender green shoots of grass sprouting along the banks of the gully. For more than an hour he chewed steadily, forcing himself to swallow the wads of green pulp.

"What's it like?" Jess asked.

He shook his head, his skin suddenly pale and pasty beneath its layer of grime. Then he pitched forward onto his knees and was violently sick.

The retching went on for a long time, his whole body shuddering with periodic convulsions. When finally the spasms passed, he was so weak he could barely sit up. Jess, squatting beside him, wiped the perspiration from his face with a damp handkerchief while the baboons looked on quizzically. Although she was genuinely sorry for him, she also felt relieved. Even David would not be able to argue this away. Painful though the experience must have been, it was at the same time a practical demonstration of their real plight, of their lack of food and provisions. There was, she felt sure, only one course open to them now.

"There," she said soothingly, "rest for a while, you'll feel better later. And tomorrow we'll get you out of here. It'll soon be over."

But once again she was to be proved wrong. For their real ordeal, as she was to discover, had only just begun.

SIX

"I don't understand why you should object," David said. "You didn't mind about stealing the Land Rover. Why is this any different?"

"Because with the Land Rover we had no option," Jess replied. "This time we have a choice."

"What? Go home? Walk out on Papio when he needs us most?"—he sounded petulant, hurt.

"That's not the only possibility."

"Oh, I see," he said sarcastically, "you're suggesting we sit here and starve."

"You know that isn't what I mean either. I just don't see the point in stealing when all we have to do is go to the farmers and ask. We're not exactly renegades. They'll give us something to eat, I'm sure."

"You mean beg for a few lousy mealies?"

"If you want to put it like that, yes."

"Well you can count me out."

He stood up, the wash of evening light falling full across his face. His nose and forehead were burned and peeling from days of exposure to the sun, patches of new skin showing pink and smooth through the accumulated dirt.

"What's the matter?" she asked. "Is begging beneath your dignity?"

"No, I just prefer my method. It's safer. No sane person goes walking into the enemy camp with a begging bowl in his hand."

It dawned on her then what he was really getting at.

"But they're not the enemy, David. They're poor farmers. It's not fair to lump them in with the people at the research unit."

"Why's that?"

"Because they have nothing to do with each other."

He laughed bitterly.

"Try taking Papio and Upi into one of the villages and you'll soon find out how wrong you are."

She fell silent, feeling hedged in by his arguments and yet at the same time unconvinced by them. Glancing up through the trees, she noticed how the sunset had spread halfway across the sky, the high strata of cloud glowing a deep and angry red, like an open wound stretching up into the heavens.

"You make it sound as though we're against everyone," she said unhappily, "as though we're engaged in a kind of war."

"Well, aren't we? How many of those people out there care a damn about Papio and Upi? We're the only ones who do, Jess."

"Maybe, but that doesn't make the rest of the population our enemies."

"What does it make them, our friends?"

"No, not that either. Just people who . . . oh, I don't know."

It seemed so hard to express what she was really feeling—a vague sense that somehow everything was getting out of hand; that what had started as a straightforward act of rescue was gradually, step by step, becoming something more.

"So are you coming with me or not?" he said, watching her face anxiously.

There was in his voice the same undertone of pleading that he had used once before and that she found so difficult to resist.

"Of course I'm coming," she responded quickly. "It's just that I wish we were going about it differently. Doing it this way makes me wonder . . . oh, sort of where it's all leading."

For the first time since the conversation had begun, he grinned at her.

"I'll tell you where it's all leading," he said. "To a really good feed."

"Yes, there is that consolation," she said, and laughed.

But secretly she felt anything but happy. A small warning tic of panic pulsed somewhere in the background; the same kind of inner alarm she had experienced as a small child whenever she had been about to step into an unlighted room.

They set out at dawn, following a game trail that meandered up the hillside. At the base of the cliff they turned to the left, to where the ascent was less steep and a zigzag path led up onto the plateau. Because of Upi, they had to take the journey in short, easy stages, so that it was mid morning by the time they reached the top.

For a while they rested in the narrow strip of bush

that separated the wild country from the settled farmland. Beneath them the vast Zambezi valley stretched away into the misty distance—the river, for all its size, showing as a thin blue-black snake winding through a velvety texture of green. The plateau, by comparison, felt unbelievably flat, the sky huge now that it was no longer viewed through a veil of trees.

"I feel as though we're at the very top of the world," Jess said, lying in the coarse grass and gazing up at the clouds.

The two baboons were less elated. They obviously felt vulnerable in this high open place and they huddled against David and Jess, yakking softly.

"Well, there it is," David said, pointing through the fringe of scrub and grass.

They could just see the beginning of the mealie fields, the bright green plants, taller than a man, growing in straight, orderly rows. Leaving David's knapsack on the lip of the escarpment, they crept through the bush to the edge of the field. Only a few yards of open ground separated them from the mealies, but they hesitated before crossing it because of a small group of thatched huts immediately to their right.

"They're pretty close," Jess said apprehensively. "How about heading farther down the field?"

"I don't know that it's worth it. There doesn't seem to be anyone around. Come on, let's take a chance."

The four of them scurried across the open ground and in among the tall plants. Here they were able to stand up without fear of being seen, the spaces between the rows like long green tunnels partly overarched by the curving leaves. The mealies themselves were not completely ripe, the strands of silk dangling from their tips only just beginning to wither and turn black. But some of them were big enough to be eaten, as Jess discovered when she twisted one from its stalk and peeled back the protective leaves.

"They'll do," David said.

Working quickly, they began tearing off the biggest they could find and stuffing them into the one knapsack they had brought with them. The two baboons, meanwhile, responded to the situation very differently. Surrounded by an abundance of food, they simply picked the first mealies at hand and started eating them then and there, biting into the half-developed kernels and the still succulent cobs with their front incisors.

"That's about as many as we can take," Jess said, forcing the zipper of the knapsack to close. "Let's get out of here."

She and David dashed back across the open ground and into the long grass. Neither baboon followed—both of them still squatting between the rows of plants, eating greedily.

"Come on, you two!" Jess hissed.

Papio grunted and half rose, but when Upi showed no readiness to leave he settled back to the unexpected feast.

"Wait here," David said, "I'll get them."

Again he scurried across the cleared ground and began urging the two animals back along the row. They moved reluctantly, grunting out in protest and snatching at mealies as they passed. Upi in particular was unhappy about having to go. She clung with both hands to one of the tall stems, and when David pushed her,

61

she flattened her ears and shook the plant vigorously.

That might have been what alerted the dogs in the village, because suddenly there was a sound of barking and four of them came pelting along the edge of the field. Papio and Upi required no urging now: In two or three bounds they had disappeared into the bush. David was not nearly so quick. Before he could regain the cover of the long grass the dogs had reached him, the leader leaping up and snapping viciously, its teeth leaving a shallow gash on his forearm.

"David!" Jess screamed.

She sprang into the open, swinging the heavy knapsack, catching one of the dogs on the side of the head and sending it tumbling. The very unexpectedness of her attack made them give ground. But only for a second or two—then they were back, forming a circle around David and Jess, snapping and barking as they closed in. One of them, a thin hollow-flanked creature, dodged past the swinging bag and bit Jess lightly on the calf, its teeth just lifting the skin. Emboldened by its success, it tried the same maneuver on David. While it was still in the act of darting forward, there was a gray-brown blur, a grating roar—and the next moment Papio was standing over the fallen animal. His lips were pulled back in a snarl, the mantle of long fur covering his neck and shoulders raised in a fierce leonine ruff. Beneath him, the dog lay still, its head thrown back, its throat bloodied and torn.

The other three hounds didn't attempt to intervene. With a series of terrified yelps they turned tail and dashed back toward the village. Papio made no effort to follow them, continuing to stand over the fallen victim, his back teeth grinding rhythmically, his tiny ears flattened against his skull.

"Papio!" David said in a shocked whisper, "Papio!"

In response to the familiar voice, the heavy mantle of fur began slowly to subside, the snarling lips to ease back over the exposed canines. Once again he was the Papio they knew: docile, obedient, slightly unsure of himself; and the body of the dog seemed a kind of mistake, something that shouldn't have been there. Papio looked down at it with his usual puzzled expression, fingered the sightless head as though he also wondered about it, why it was so warm, yet so still.

"What have you . . .?" Jess began.

At that moment a shot rang out, seemingly right behind them, and in a flash Papio was gone. Jess and David, still too shocked to run, turned to find themselves confronted by two figures: an old African man and a young boy of approximately their own age. The man, dressed only in a pair of baggy shorts, was tall and thin and so old that the flesh hung from his bones in soft brown folds. His hair was sparse and completely white, his eyes bloodshot and rheumy from years of exposure to bright sunlight. Beside him, the boy appeared amazingly young and fresh-faced. He stood close to the old man who leaned one hand heavily on his shoulder. In the other gnarled fist was a rifle, a battered Lee Enfield nearly as old as himself.

He waved it now in the direction of the departed baboons, talking angrily in Nyanja, looking alternately from Jess to the fallen dog.

"I'm sorry, but I don't speak your language," Jess said in a small voice. "I'm from the United States."

The old man paused and gently shook the boy's shoulder. The boy answered him in Nyanja and then said in faltering English:

"My grandfather say, why you come with this animals? Why you kill dog?"

He had, Jess noticed, soft intelligent eyes and none of the ferocity and belligerence of the old man.

"We're sorry about the dog," she said, "we really are." She glanced at the dead body and quickly turned her back on it, feeling slightly sickened by the sight. "We never dreamed that might happen. You see, Papio isn't a wild baboon. He's really tame. They both are. That's why we never thought . . ."

She stole another hurried glance over her shoulder and looked apologetically at the old man who made a disapproving, clicking sound with his tongue and shook his head sadly.

"And please tell him," Jess went on in a rush, "that we didn't really want to steal anything. We're sorry about that too. But we've been living in the bush for a week and we've run out of food."

The boy, who had been struggling to follow her, nodded understandingly and began translating. A brief discussion took place and slowly the anger seemed to melt out of the old man. He let the rifle slip through his fingers until he was holding it by the muzzle, using it now more as a support than a weapon. Regarding Jess and David with a new interest, he gave what sounded like a series of instructions.

"He say you come now to the village," the boy explained. "We are cooking for you." He pressed the fingers of one hand together and pointed to his mouth, afterward patting his belly. "Plenty nshima, plenty good kapenta, for eating."

He smiled, pleased with his own description—but before Jess could answer, David took her by the arm.

"No, we can't stay," he said.

"Perhaps just for a while . . . ?" Jess suggested.

He released her arm and shrugged indifferently, already half turned away.

"Please yourself. I'm going after Papio."

He gazed down at the dog lying at his feet and touched it with his toe. He seemed vaguely concerned by what had happened, but Jess sensed that it was more for Papio's sake than for the dog's.

"Are you coming or stopping here?" he added.

She hesitated, feeling embarrassed by his attitude and also vaguely resentful of what he was again forcing onto her. Finally she said to the boy:

"Please tell your grandfather that I'm grateful, but I have to . . ." She almost admitted it then—the truth, that David was her only reason for leaving. "I mean we have to stay with the animals," she added quickly.

Again the man and boy spoke together. This time they sounded as though they were arguing, and when the boy turned back to her he appeared less happy.

"My grandfather, he say, you forget dog. Is finished. For today, you take this mealies." He pointed to the bulging satchel. "Tomorrow, you are coming now-now. We give hot food. Here, in this place. Not village. You are taking food far away. Tomorrow, you understand?"

"Yes, we understand, don't we, David?"

"I suppose so," he murmured grudgingly.

He was beginning to shuffle toward the long grass.

"And we will come tomorrow?"

Without bothering to answer, he turned and slipped back into the bush, moving almost like a furtive animal. Reluctantly, Jess followed him, pausing at the edge of the cleared ground and glancing once more, painfully, at the dead animal stretched out on the dry earth.

"We'll be here, I promise," she said.

The old man smiled at her, showing an even row of worn teeth, and waved his free hand encouragingly. The boy still appeared not so much unhappy as ill at ease, a frown creasing his forehead.

"Tomorrow," he said mechanically, his eyes lowered, refusing to look at her.

"I don't like it," David muttered.

"I know that," Jess answered, "but you won't explain why. Come on, what's wrong with going back?"

"I just don't like it, that's all."

He leaned forward and tended the fire on which they had cooked their evening meal. It flared briefly, revealing the ghostly shapes of trees through which a newly risen moon gazed balefully at them. Overhead, Papio and Upi stirred as the light from the flames flickered among the branches.

"If you think about it," Jess said, "they're the ones who should be suspicious. We arrive out of nowhere like a couple of savages, we steal their crops, and then we kill one of their dogs. How would you feel in their position?"

"It wasn't our fault about the dog," he muttered.

"I'm not so sure about that. I seem to remember we came out here to try and keep animals alive. Now there's a dead body lying up there. It must be partly our fault."

"It could just as easily have been Papio's body."

"That's not the point."

"I guess not."

They were silent for several minutes, gazing thoughtfully into the flames.

"I still don't see why you're keen to go back," he said quietly.

"Well, we have to leave here eventually," she began, but he glanced away evasively. "All right," she went on, "I guess I want to go back to the village because they were so nice, offering to help us out after what we'd done. We do need some help—food and things—and it's too good an offer to turn down."

"It is, if you believe them."

Jess blew out her lips irritably.

"You know your trouble, David? You're becoming paranoid. You think everyone's trying to get you."

He fingered the handkerchief tied around the flesh wound on his arm. Somewhere out in the darkness a nightjar called plaintively.

"There must be quite a few people looking for us by now," he said.

"Yes, but not the whole country. Not everyone."

"No, not everyone," he conceded. "That boy, he was probably all right."

"So what's worrying you about tomorrow?"

"I think maybe it's the old man. I don't trust him."

"But what can he do to us?"

"He does have a gun."

Again Jess huffed irritably.

"He could have used that today if he'd wanted. Why didn't he?"

"I don't know. It's this feeling I have."

"Well, forget it. I did promise them, and we have to start trusting people some time."

"I just hope we don't both regret it," he said ominously.

Those words came back to Jess later that night as she lay curled up beside the fire. Secretly she didn't wholly disagree with David. Despite her apparent confidence, she could not forget the African boy's refusal to meet her eyes right at the end of their meeting. There was a risk in going back—she admitted that to herself. But there was perhaps an even bigger risk in staying away, because more than anything else she was frightened of remaining totally cut off from other people. She couldn't bear to think of their present isolation going on day after day, with no definite end in sight. Although she could not exactly say why, such a possibility appalled her. Anything, she felt, was preferable to it. And with that conviction she fell asleep.

When she awoke in the morning the fire had been out for some time, with the result that her face and the backs of her hands were covered with mosquito bites. Her forehead felt bumpy to the touch and both eyes were so badly swollen that she could barely see.

"I feel like a wreck," she said, rising stiffly to her feet.

She nearly added that she could not stand much more of living like this, but she choked the words back, placing her trust in the day ahead.

David had also been badly bitten, and yet he seemed not to notice the discomfort. He was nervous and edgy, eager for them to be off.

"Come on," he said, "let's get it over with."

Jess, for different reasons, was just as eager, and without even a light breakfast to sustain them, they began the upward journey.

Because they had not traveled far down the slope on the previous day, they reached the edge of the plateau slightly ahead of time. Jess was all for going straight to the huts, but David was more cautious.

"No," he insisted, "we keep out of sight and wait."

So for more than an hour they crouched in the long grass next to the field, giving no indication of their presence.

Shortly after mid morning, the old man and the boy emerged from the ring of huts. Neither of them was armed and they were carrying two large calabash gourds. The boy was also holding a bundle of mealies tied together with string. Not until they were well away from the village did David and Jess step out into the open. The old man immediately smiled, placed his calabash on the ground, and brought both hands up to his forehead in greeting. Then, pointing invitingly to the open mouth of the calabash, he motioned for them to approach.

Jess went without hesitation, David following her more cautiously. She was on the point of turning to him, of exclaiming how right she had been, when all at once she noticed something that stopped her in her tracks. There was no steam rising from the mouths of the calabashes, even though the boy had spoken to them of hot food.

"Wait!" she hissed.

Almost in the same instant Upi barked a warning from her hiding place in the long grass.

"It's a trap!" David yelled.

He turned and dashed back into the bush, leaving Jess standing alone on the open ground. Already men dressed in khaki were running from the village. There was a swish of leaves and a thud of heavy footsteps as more men crashed their way across the field.

"Quick! This way!" David shouted.

Still she didn't move. It was for Jess a time of bitter decision. For the space of a few agonizing seconds she stood poised, torn between the desire to give herself up, for all this to be over, and her equally strong need to remain with David, not to let him disappear, alone, back into all that darkness and confusion. If, at that moment, someone had only called her by name and so reminded her of the warm world of home that lay beyond this field, she would probably have stayed, have settled for her own comfort and security. But all that happened was that one of the advancing men bawled out:

"Hey you! Stay where you are!"

She moved then, taking one or two hesitant steps, and pausing yet again, still not totally decided, looking now at the boy, her eyes begging him for help. He didn't speak to her—he merely smiled, meeting her eyes at last, and with a deft movement of his wrist tossed the bundle of mealies toward her. In all the panic and confusion that one small action passed unnoticed. But for Jess it was a clear sign—not only of what she should do, but somehow of the rightness of her intended action. In a way, it was also an indication of the peculiar rightness of David's, and even of her own, supposedly darker impulses. There was no opportunity to sort out this jumble of thoughts—she knew only that she must act while she still had the chance.

"Thank you," she said impulsively.

And scooping up the bundle, she turned and ran.

By now the men were not far behind her, but she had no difficulty in outdistancing them, her long thin legs carrying her effortlessly over the uneven ground. At the edge of the plateau she gathered up the knapsack she had left there, and then she was leaping and sliding down the steep zigzag path.

She caught up with David and the baboons near the bottom. Upi, pushed to the limit, had collapsed completely. She was lying on her back, her jaws gaping as she fought for breath.

"We'll have to carry her!" David said desperately.

"What about the food and stuff? Do we ditch it?"

"No, Papio can bring it for us."

Much to Papio's surprise, they hung the two knapsacks around his neck and thrust the bundle of mealies into his arms. He grunted disapprovingly but accepted the burden, looking on as they heaved Upi up between them and hurried down the slope.

For the first few minutes they managed to keep moving fairly easily. Gradually, however, they began to tire, and soon they were covered in sweat and staggering under Upi's weight. What made matters worse, they had failed to throw off their pursuers. Each time they paused to rest, the shouts of the men sounded closer.

"It's no use," Jess said, "this isn't going to work."

They lowered Upi to the ground. She was still far too distressed to walk or run.

"There's only one thing for it," David said, "we'll

have to backtrack and try to lead them away from the animals."

But even that was impossible now, because their pursuers were too close. David began scrambling back up the hillside, realized the futility of what he hoped to do, and stopped. Near to where he was standing were several rocks lying loose on the ground, and he picked up one about the size of his fist. With his face pale and tense, he stood hefting it in his hand, waiting.

"That won't do any good!" Jess whispered fiercely.

"We'll see about that."

"You'll just make everything worse."

"It can't be any worse—not if they take Papio and Upi back."

His sullen determination alarmed her almost as much as the shouts of the men on the hillside, and she went over and tried to wrench the rock from his grasp. The two of them struggled silently for a moment. With an effort, he pulled himself free and pushed her roughly to one side, again advancing up the slope.

"David," she pleaded, "that's not the way."

The men were so close that Jess could hear their footsteps on the hard ground. Before they came into view a loud bark rang out on the ridge over to their right. Jess spun around, saw Papio was still with them, and realized it was the troop of wild baboons that they hadn't heard for several days. Above them, the footsteps had stopped. The bark came again and a voice shouted:

"Over there."

To their relief the men veered away, the footsteps and shouts growing rapidly fainter.

David dropped the rock and came back to where Upi was struggling up onto all fours.

"What luck," he said, wiping the sweat from his forehead. "We'll let Upi rest for a while, then make our way further down, into the heavy bush along the gullies."

Jess stood up slowly.

"I don't think that's a very good idea," she said.

"Why not?"

"Because in five or six days we'll be out of food, and this whole business will start again."

"So what? We'll be more careful next time."

"There isn't going to be a next time."

He swung quickly toward her.

"Look, I'm sorry about shoving you . . ."

"It isn't that," she interrupted, "it's what might have happened if they'd come down here. Have you thought about that—of the way Papio might have reacted if you'd tried to fight them off? You saw him with the dogs yesterday."

"Papio would never attack a human being."

"God, David, how do you know?"

"But I've told you," he said desperately, "we'll be more careful in the future."

She waved the idea aside scornfully, the two of them confronting each other over the still gasping body of Upi—two dirty, ragged figures, their clothes torn, their wounds of the previous day bound up with pieces of filthy handkerchief, their faces puffy and swollen from mosquito bites.

"Just look at us," Jess said less excitedly, "at the state we're in."

He made a halfhearted attempt to laugh.

"You do look a bit of a mess."

"I wouldn't mind so much if we'd achieved anything. But we haven't, have we? Be honest."

"We've been doing our best," he said defensively.

"And our best hasn't been good enough."

"So what's next? Are you saying we should pack it in? Because if that's your attitude . . ."

Again she cut him short, her voice determined, decisive.

"I wouldn't have run away from those men if I'd thought that. No, you're right about finishing what we've begun. That's why we have to change our tactics. We have to make it so Papio and Upi won't ever need us again."

He bent down, hovering protectively over Upi, his fingers gently caressing the soft fur beneath her chin.

"I suppose you've worked out some fiendish master plan," he said, an edge of sarcasm in his voice.

"Not a master plan—just common sense. She pointed toward the ridge where the sharp barks of fleeing baboons could still be heard. "Listen to that. Doesn't it mean something to you?"

"I don't follow you."

"Then keep listening."

He gave her a puzzled glance.

"What's all that noise got to do with anything? It's just a crowd of men chasing a troop of baboons."

"That's right," she said with a smile. "And they won't catch them, will they?"

SEVEN

It rained for the first time in a week that evening: not a heavy storm, but sufficient to scour out the muddy holes in the gullies and leave them brimming with fresh water. After the initial downpour, a light misty rain continued to drift across the hillside for some hours, and Jess and David spent much of the night huddled together in a makeshift shelter over which they had spread the plastic raincoat. Toward morning the sky cleared, and just as dawn was breaking they left their shelter and made their way to the top of the nearest ridge. With the surrounding forest still deep in shadow, they looked up toward the cliffs that were already streaked with bright yellow sunlight.

"They'll be awake and moving by now," Jess said. "Can you make your voice carry that far?"

"I think so."

Cupping his hands around his mouth, he made the loud explosive bark that baboons use whenever they are alarmed. Papio, who was sitting beside them, shifted uncomfortably, his lips drawing back from his teeth in a nervous grimace, but there was no answering call from the cliffs.

"Try again," Jess urged him.

David repeated the sound with the same negative result.

"Never mind," she said, "if we're patient we'll catch up with them sooner or later. After the scare they had yesterday they probably moved off to another part of their territory."

As she spoke, the sun appeared above the horizon, sending thin shafts of light stabbing between the trees. Upi, who like all baboons was frightened of the dark, grunted with approval and immediately began the day-long search for food. David watched both her and Papio saunter down the slope, nibbling at plants and turning over rocks as they went.

"And you really think the troop will accept them?" he said.

"Maybe not right away, but they will eventually."

"Why do they have to?"

"Because they're the same species, and all animals accept their own kind—especially when they're friendly animals, like baboons."

He rubbed his hand slowly across his face—an odd gesture that Jess found difficult to interpret.

"Human beings don't always accept their own kind," he. said. "Sometimes they even reject people who . . . who they're supposed to be fond of."

She gave a short, forced laugh.

"Ah, but human beings are a special sort of animal. They aren't faithful and dependable like baboons."

It was meant as a joke, but David seemed to take it seriously.

"Yes, I suppose that's it," he said, and clambered down

to where Papio was digging for tubers in the rain-wet soil.

Throughout the rest of that day they traveled slowly eastward. At regular intervals David repeated the warning bark, but all that ever came back to them was a dim echo from the steep face of the escarpment.

By evening he was sick of calling and began to grumble about how they were wasting their time. Yet as Jess pointed out, there was no other real alternative—and in any case the day had not been a total loss. Ever since the attack on the dog, Papio seemed to have been undergoing some form of transformation, as though that bloody incident had shocked him out of his dullness, stirring within him some forgotten conception of himself. The puzzled expression in his eyes had begun to fade, and now, whether they were resting or on the move, he was the one who stood guard over the group. In times of trouble—such as when Upi encountered a snake and screamed out a warning, her fur standing on end with fright—he still ran to David, but he was no longer seeking comfort and protection. He had become the protector, ready to interpose himself between his companions and any possible enemy.

"Do you think he'll be like his old self eventually?" David asked as they sat around the camp fire that night.

"Who knows? His instincts are certainly coming back. As for his mind . . . we'll have to wait and see."

David picked up a length of twig and snapped it in two, tossing the pieces into the fire and watching them flare up.

"What if his mind never clears?" he said.

"As long as he's with his own kind, it won't matter.

That's why we have to find the troop. If he's part of a big group, he won't have to think for himself and make decisions; he'll share their collective wisdom. They'll take our place."

"Yes, there is that possibility," he said vaguely.

Only minutes later he lay down with his head on Jess's lap, snuggling against her even though the night was warm. He was soon asleep, in the manner of a small child, falling straight into the peace and darkness of oblivion. And Jess, as was so often the case now, was left to keep a lonely vigil. She stroked his hair lightly, not yet ready for sleep, gazing past the flames into the night. A week earlier, in a similar situation, she had been able to think only of her home, of the sustaining warmth and affection of her family. Now, her mind kept turning to the idea of the baboon troop, refusing to consider anything beyond that one fixed notion—clinging to it as to a lifeline in the storm and turbulence of strange seas.

It was David's idea to climb the tree. With Papio shadowing his every move, he clambered up through the lower branches, pulling himself from limb to limb until he was level with the surrounding canopy. Papio was unwilling to go further than that. As soon as the branches began to sway beneath his weight, he held on tightly and refused to budge. But David pushed on, ignoring Papio's anxious grunts, shinnying up the swaying limbs to a point where he could gaze out over the countryside.

"What can you see?" Jess's voice floated up to him, slightly muffled by the canopy.

Wedging himself securely into a three-pronged fork of branches, he looked toward the north. It was unlikely that the troop would still be sheltering in the less accessible heights, and he concentrated on the slope below the cliffs. It was mainly rocky and bare, supporting only a few knobthorn bushes and a scattering of giant aloes. At that time of morning the shadows were long, the few plants casting spiky black lines across the rocky surface. He thought for a minute that was all there was, just the strips of shadow traversing the stony face of the slope—but then he caught a glimpse of movement . . . and another! And suddenly he saw them—so well camouflaged that they melted into even that inhospitable background—a whole troop of baboons picking their way across the hillside.

"There they are!" he called.

He slid rapidly down the tree, grazing his shins and half falling the last six feet.

"How many?" Jess asked excitedly.

"It's hard to say. A hundred, maybe more."

Right away they headed in a northeasterly direction, hoping to cut the troop off. It was impossible to hurry, because of Upi, but they kept up a steady pace and shortly before midday David succeeded in establishing voice contact. That first response, a hoarse coughing bark, had little effect on Papio and Upi who had grown used to such cries over the past week. As the bark became louder and closer they began to take more of an interest, their bodies quivering with alertness, their eyes scanning the way ahead. Soon it was unnecessary for David to call out in order to pinpoint the troop's whereabouts. Upi, prompted by her natural curiosity and her usual sure sense of what was expected of her, forged ahead, leading the way. Panting heavily, but never pushing herself to the point of collapse, she chose a path that brought them up with the troop in the early afternoon.

That first encounter was not encouraging. The troop was feeding with a small herd of impala whose keen sense of smell enabled them to give an early warning, and all Jess and David saw were a few gray-brown shapes disappearing between the trees.

"Damn!" Jess exclaimed impatiently.

David bent over one of the pools in the depths of the gully and splashed water onto his face.

"Don't worry," he said, squeezing water from his eyes, "it's a start. At least they know we're here now."

They set out again, in spite of the gathering heat, and this time, without any prompting from David, Papio took the lead. That contact with the troop, brief though it had been, seemed to have triggered something inside him— perhaps even touched his slowly awakening intelligence, for he now gave every indication of understanding their purpose. This was evident not only in the way he led them straight to the troop, but also in the caution he displayed. Just before their presence could be detected, he stopped, peered suspiciously at the surrounding bush, and then advanced far more slowly and carefully.

With a fitful breeze blowing directly in their faces, they crept over a slight rise and saw the main body of the troop feeding peacefully below them. There was an assortment of animals: babies clinging to the undersides of their mothers or riding jockey-fashion on their mothers' backs; juveniles sitting in groups or frolicking together; and several large males. One male in particular stood out from the rest. He was a magnificent animal, almost as big as Papio, and the way he moved among the others made it clear that he stepped aside for no one. As they watched, he stopped beside two females who immediately gave up feeding in order to groom him.

"He must be the leader," David whispered.

"He's more like a sultan in his harem."

"Yes, the sultan."

There was a low, breathy grunt from Papio, as though he too were trying to express his views. Jess grinned and urged him and Upi forward.

"Come on," she said, "time for introductions."

She gave them both a friendly shove and crouched beside David to observe the events. The two baboons walked cautiously into the open and sat down. It took only a few seconds for the troop to notice them. There was no general outcry, nor even any great show of interest. Several of the juveniles and infants made a high-pitched clicking sound and moved closer to the adults, but that was all. Papio and Upi, apparently unconcerned, rose and sauntered forward, turning over sticks and stones in their path as though unaware of the troop. And still nothing happened—until Papio seemed to cross some invisible line. Then the big leader whom Jess and David had christened Sultan stalked through the troop toward them. Two others joined him, one on either side—another large male with some kind of skin disorder, because there were hairless, rough patches all over his chest and arms; and a smaller animal, lean in the body, but with powerful shoulders. These three advanced to within a few yards of the intruders and took up a threatening posture, their shoulders thrust forward aggressively. Yet even now they showed no signs of wanting to charge, and Papio and Upi in turn made no attempt to retreat—they merely displayed the kind of nervous behavior Jess and David had witnessed scores of times before. Upi gave an uncertain grin, drawing her lips jerkily back from her teeth, meanwhile turning aside almost shyly; and Papio yawned, afterward staring blankly up into space.

"It looks as though it's going to work!" Jess whispered excitedly.

David raised a finger to his lips, but his warning came too late. The baboons, already alerted by the intrusion, must have heard her voice, because the broad-shouldered male skittered to one side and leapt up onto a half-rotted log. From there he had a full view of the human intruders and instantly he gave the alarm. What had been a peaceful scene exploded into frantic activity as baboons scrambled up into trees. Only the three males didn't retreat right away: They backed off slowly, allowing the rest of the troop to escape, turning and running only when the few stragglers were safely clear. Sultan went last of all, giving a single, defiant bark before he too vanished into the undergrowth.

"Sorry about that," Jess said. "I thought their eyesight was their strong point, but old Muscles there, the one with the shoulders, would have heard a twig snap at a hundred yards."

David walked over and fondled Papio's head, rubbing his fingers lightly over the electrodes that shone in the sunlight.

"Their eyesight's what they rely on most, but their hearing's pretty good."

"Now he tells me," Jess said, and laughed.

He smiled back at her and she added quickly:

"What do you say to moving on?"

"If you like."

He sounded as vague and unenthusiastic as he had all along, but Jess suspected that, as with Papio a few minutes earlier, his indifference was more feigned than real—that the process of making contact with the troop had begun to intrigue him.

In the hours that followed they caught up with the troop several times, and on every occasion the animals scampered off. Each successive flight, however, was less frantic than the one before. The baboons always ran for safety, but they did so with increasing reluctance, more irritated than positively frightened. During the final encounter, late in the afternoon, many of the animals actually remained in the treetops, barking indignantly as Jess and David passed beneath them.

Jess stopped and peered upward, unable to spot any movement, yet curiously aware of the many eyes watching her.

"We're not the only ones who are learning," she said, harking back to an earlier conversation. "They know already we aren't going to hurt them. By this time tomorrow they probably won't mind us, provided we don't come too close. That's all we need. After that . . ."

Before she could finish, Sultan's defiant roar drowned out every other sound, and a powerful figure ran nimbly along the branch directly above her head.

It was the worst time of day—the hottest part of a stifling afternoon. Earlier, thunderheads had gathered on the horizon, circled promisingly, and been swept away, leaving the air humid and still, alive with the unwavering shriek of cicadas. From where she lay, in the patchy shade of grass and thornbush, Jess could see the troop clearly. They were resting in the shelter of a giant fig tree. Some of them were sprawled out or grooming in the deep shadow, while others had climbed up over the massive buttress of roots and were sitting in the forks of branches.

"Now's our chance," she said quietly. "They won't run in this heat, not when it means leaving a comfortable spot."

Shepherding the two baboons before them, she and David crept closer, approaching to within fifty yards without being spotted. At that point the bush thinned to little more than light scrub. The cause of this was the fig tree itself, whose vast root system had spread out over a wide circumference, robbing the surrounding area of water and nourishment.

"You're on your own from here," Jess murmured to the two animals.

They sauntered forward as they had several times before—with feigned nonchalance, yawning extravagantly and glancing from side to side. When they were still less than halfway to the tree they stopped and looked back.

"Keep moving," Jess urged them, mouthing the words silently and flapping her hands.

That action alone was enough to attract attention,

and a few animals, from their lookout posts in the tree, let out feeble barks—intended not so much to alert the troop as to warn the intruders off. Encouraged by their lassitude, Jess stepped into the open and again urged Papio and Upi on. There were a few more barks, but no move to sound a general alarm. On the other hand, neither Papio nor Upi showed any readiness to leave their human companions and mingle with the troop. Stranded in a kind of no-man's-land equidistant between the two groups, they idly fingered the dry soil and clumps of grass, periodically scratching themselves and yawning in what looked like a display of boredom but was in reality a sign of anxiety and indecision.

"What's with them?" Jess said, exasperated.

David had crawled silently up beside her.

"They don't know how to choose," he murmured. "They want to be with the troop and stay with us too."

Jess shook her head with frustration. There were beads of sweat across her upper lip and in the hollows around her eyes. She appeared not only hot and tired, but also unnaturally distraught, as though she were near the end of her rope.

"They can't have it both ways!" she said, her voice growing shrill.

"They don't see it like that, Jess."

"Then I'll soon show them!"

Rising to her feet, she marched boldly across to Papio and Upi.

"Get over there!" she shouted. "Go on, move! They're baboons, the same as . . ."

What happened next was so unexpected that it caught them all by surprise. There was a challenging roar, and

Sultan, who until then had been sitting quietly in the shade, came charging across the open ground. The two senior males who had previously lent him support also burst from cover, but theirs were only mock charges that petered out after a few strides. Not so with Sultan. He actually gathered pace—his head thrust forward, his eyes staring, his jaw gaping wide.

Jess, looking up quickly, saw with horror that he was charging not at the group in general, but specifically at her—the direct line of his run leading past Upi to where she was standing. She let out a scream of genuine terror and threw her hands up defensively, her whole body braced for the impact.

Yet it never came. Papio, with the same astonishing speed he had displayed once before, leapt straight into Sultan's path. No longer the shy, diffident animal who seconds earlier had crouched timidly in the sunlight, he now met the troop leader's charge with an equal degree of ferocity—the two heavy bodies colliding in midair and whirling over and over as they bit and slashed at each other.

The savage combat lasted for only a few seconds, but when they parted they were both bleeding: Sultan from a torn lip, Papio from a light wound on the neck. Now they stood only a foot or two apart, on all fours, their mantles raised, their shoulders hunched and straining forward. Both were grinding their teeth and raising their eyebrows, with low menacing grunts coming from Sultan as he threatened to renew the attack.

Jess, deeply shaken, was still standing with her arms upraised, too shocked to move. She was aware that David was saying something to her, but the words themselves meant nothing. She felt his hands grasp her from behind.

"It's us," he was whispering, "he doesn't like us so close."

She allowed herself to be led backward. And once again it was as though there were an invisible line that Sultan had decided upon, because after Jess had taken only a few stumbling steps, his mantle hair slowly subsided and, turning away, he stalked back to the huge tree. Papio also reverted to his former role, scratching casually at the sandy soil and nervously wiping his muzzle with one hand before following Upi, who was already ambling toward Jess and David.

"Whew! That was close!" David said. "Are you all right?"

Instead of answering, she pulled away from him and dashed off into the bush, dropping her knapsack in her haste. Ignoring the stiff clumps of grass that scratched her legs, or the branches of thorn trees that tore at her arms and hair, she ran blindly, fleeing rapidly through a patchwork of sunlight and shade; stumbling and sometimes falling, but staggering on again; running and running until she could hardly breathe, her face and body streaming with sweat. Only then, when she no longer had the energy to keep going, did she slow reluctantly to a walk and finally sink forward onto her hands and knees, her breath coming in great sobbing gasps that sounded as much like grief as exhaustion.

It took David and the two animals nearly ten minutes to find her. She was sitting in a sun-speckled glade, her hands over her face. There were deep scratches on her bare skin, but it wasn't those David noticed. Rather it was the streaks of tears that had run between her fingers and scored silty channels through the dirt and dust covering her hands and wrists. He had never seen her like this before; it was as if some secret, childlike side of Jess's nature, previously suppressed, had been forced to the surface at a moment of deep stress. And the sudden revelation of this younger, less adult Jess had a steadying effect on him; it made him, by comparison, feel older, more responsible.

Squatting beside her, he smoothed down her hair that had been teased out into a wild tangle by the overhanging branches of thorn trees; then, still without speaking, he began picking off the tiny black-brown ticks that clung to her ankles and to the tattered denim of her pants.

Gradually he felt her grow calmer, the peace and silence of the surrounding bush settling upon them. Near the edge of the glade Papio and Upi were browsing quietly. Above their heads there was an intermittent stirring amid the foliage as a flock of white-eyes searched for insects. In a nearby tree a weaver bird, long black tail trailing, surveyed the scene below.

She drew her hands slowly away from her face and stared blankly at the ground, where a line of ants was toiling steadily across what was for them a rough, forbidding terrain.

"I don't know what to do anymore," she said tearfully. "Nothing seems to work. It's all a stupid mess. Stupid!"

She expected David to act defensively, but he merely moved around so he could see her face.

"There's nothing stupid about what we're doing, Jess,"

he said gently. "Really. And your idea of getting them to join the troop is the best part. It's worth all the struggle and even that fright you had back there, because it makes sense of everything. It's what has to happen whether we like it or not."

She thought for a moment that he was just placating her.

"You don't really want them to join the troop, though, do you?"

He dropped a piece of stick onto the ground, directly in the path of the ants, watching as they struggled to find a way over it, straining and tugging at the tiny seeds and fragments of leaf they were taking back to their nest.

"In a way, maybe I do," he said. "Just now, when Papio and Sultan were fighting, I was scared, but that wasn't all. Looking at them like that, face to face, I couldn't help thinking how similar they were—Sultan, a kind of older version of Papio; the way Papio will be when he's spent a year or so here . . . no, not just here, I mean among his own kind."

"If he ever gets the chance."

"Oh, he will."

"Why are you so sure?"

"Because . . ."—he hesitated, grinning at her. "Perhaps it's an instinct I've developed from living in the bush."

"Be serious."

"Don't call it an instinct then. But d'you remember the feeling I had about going back to the village? Well, I have the opposite feeling about this place. I know in the end everything will be all right here. It's not like being at home, among people. There's something about this place—the bush, the animals, everything—that you can . . . can sort of depend on . . . trust."

Without realizing why, Jess began to cry again. She didn't want to, but the tears forced themselves out, coursing down her grimy cheeks and forming small pools in the corners of her mouth.

"I'm sorry . . ." she stammered, ". . . stupid . . . just stupid . . ."

She tried to cover her face again, but David took her hands and pulled her toward him. It was meant as an act of comfort—David taking care of her as she had grown used to taking care of him, taking some of her former responsibilities upon himself. A reversal of roles so unexpected and startling that she found herself scrambling to her feet.

"I promise, Jess," he said, "it'll all work out. You know, what we always wanted: Papio and Upi alive and free."

"Yes," she said vaguely, and then with sudden emphasis: "Yes! Yes, I know!"

All the time thinking, with relief: It's David, the old David, come back again. Exactly the way he used to be.

Not until much later in the day did it occur to her that what had happened was far more complex than that. They were watching the sun sink through a flaming ring of cloud, the bush hushed and still at the onset of evening, a place of such peace and beauty that, much to her own surprise, she could not imagine herself wanting to be anywhere else. It was then she understood that the change had not only been in David; there had been a change in herself as well.

Something had happened to her that afternoon. Her near encounter with death, when she had faced the charging Sultan, had not left her yearning for the safety and security of home. On the contrary, it had made her home seem that much farther away, that much less real. The sheer intensity of her experience, unlike anything she had ever known before, had served only to draw her closer to her immediate surroundings. It had jolted her awake, forcing her to recognize that the bush was not something she could take for granted or simply tolerate. Her terror, in its own disturbing way, had begun the process of binding her to this bushland setting— much as love and duty had once bound her to family and home.

Jess herself was only vaguely conscious of these changes taking place within her. Still she understood enough to realize that the events of the afternoon had been nothing less than a turning point, a break with the past. A time she could look back to and say: That was where it happened, where I took a completely new direction.

Weeks later she would understand something more: that it was neither the only, nor even the most important, change she had undergone. Even so, it was a turning point, the beginning of a new phase.

"Yes," she said again, echoing her sentiments of the afternoon while the evening shadows spread rapidly through the forest all about them, "it'll be all right if we give it a chance."

EIGHT

What David and Jess had overlooked, or forgotten, was the *way* things could happen within the isolated, often savage world of the wild escarpment country.

They were camped beside a small permanent stream. For several days they had been following the troop, never making the kind of friendly contact they hoped for, yet with that invisible circle, within which Sultan would not tolerate them, growing steadily smaller. So that toward the end of that particular afternoon they had managed to approach within twenty yards of the animals. Papio and Upi had actually mingled with the young females and juveniles who played or fed on the fringes of the group.

Now the troop had taken refuge for the night in a clump of tall fever trees that grew on a level section of ground close to the stream. David and Jess, still with Papio and Upi trailing behind them, had withdrawn a short distance upstream to cook their evening meal. For a change they were not relying on mealies, which in any case they were running short of. Instead, they had a collection of birds' eggs, carefully gathered throughout the day, and a small grisly heap of dead fledgelings that Upi, with her usual uncanny ability to understand what was needed, had brought to them during the course of the afternoon. Jess had at first wanted to reject them, pained at the sight of the small pathetic bodies; but David had insisted that they accept whatever food the bush afforded. He had cleaned the tiny bodies, spitted them on green sticks, and roasted them over the fire until they were crispy brown. And Jess, despite her earlier misgivings, had eaten her share readily enough.

It was dark by the time they had finished their meal. They could hear, not far away, the restless murmurings of the troop settling for the night. In the distance there was a steady rumble of thunder as a storm crashed its way across the plateau. The thunder and lightning drew steadily nearer, and it was not long before storm clouds were looming over the escarpment and blotting out the stars. For an hour, rain lashed down, extinguishing the fire and driving David and Jess into the half-hollowed-out trunk of an old baobab tree. They remained there even after the rain had stopped. At least it was dry, and with the rest of the forest soaking wet there was no chance of relighting their fire. Huddled together in the confined space, they settled themselves for what they thought would be a long peaceful night.

The first disturbance occurred soon after they had dozed off. Papio and Upi, perched in nearby trees, gave a few nervous grunts and shifted further along the branches on which they had been sleeping. David half woke and called up drowsily:

"It's all right, you two, we're still here."

But his voice, usually enough to soothe them at night, had no effect, their grunts growing into a series of yakking cries.

David sat up and woke Jess.

"What's going on?" she asked, rubbing her eyes and staring out into the blackness.

The two animals were climbing higher up the tree, continuing to call shrilly.

"There must be something frightening them," David said.

"Yes, but what?"

Jess had no sooner framed the question than a low snarling growl issued from the darkness. Cooped up in the tree as they were, it was impossible to tell from which direction it had come. Nor did they waste time trying to find out; together, they groped around for the knapsacks, rummaging rapidly through them in search of flashlights.

Jess found hers first and clicked it on, sending a pale circle of light darting out into the night. Within that circle, shadowy and blurred at the edges, they saw the clean curve of a young tree and a green latticework of leaves and branches. Then, for a split second only, just beyond the transparent screen of sparse foliage, a flash of reflected light as two eyes met, held the beam of the flashlight, and were quickly gone.

"Leopard!"

David eased the word out softly, his voice so low that it merged with the throaty growl that was repeated—a little closer—followed almost immediately by a scrabbling on the outer shell of their refuge as the beast clawed its way up the trunk to the fork above their heads. They heard the heavy body settle among the litter of leaves and twigs that had collected there, heard the heavy, even breathing. The sound of that breathing seemed to fill the night, and everything else was stilled by it. Even Papio and Upi were temporarily

silent, clinging to each other high in the trees, as petrified as the two humans.

Nothing happened for a while after that: Jess and
David were sitting bolt upright, the flashlight in Jess's
hand trembling so violently that the beam of light shifted
and swirled like some drunken phantom. And all the
time the breathing went on, regular, deep—disturbed
at last by another of the growls, louder and more
threatening. Before it had died away, Upi let out a
screech of terror and sheer loathing, and she and Papio
began scrambling from tree to tree, leaping recklessly
through the darkness.

Jess and David, listening intently from below, heard
the two baboons escaping, their cries diminishing and
becoming less frantic as they increased the distance between themselves and the most hated of all their natural enemies. But the humans didn't dare move, the
leopard still there, crouching above them. There was a
rustle of leaves and a further scraping as it slid down
the trunk. Again it appeared, at the limit of the flashlight beam, its eyes glowing like alien moons, its low-
slung body so close to the ground that it seemed to
glide rather than walk. The leopard paused within the
pale wavering light this time, its whiskered lips crinkling back as it snarled at them; and then, more terri-
fying still, it vanished back into the shadows. Yet it did
not depart altogether, for only a few seconds later, per-
ilously close to the tree, a breaking twig cracked sharply
in the darkness.

"We have to do something!" Jess croaked, her mouth
and throat so dry that she could barely get the words
out.

The low snarl was heard once more—to their ears

like sinister, demented laughter—and the sound of a body brushing lightly, tantalizingly, against the shell of the tree.

"A fire!" David whispered. "It won't come near fire!"

He renewed his hectic search through his knapsack, succeeded in finding the second flashlight, and cast the beam around the interior of the tree. There were enough dry leaves and pieces of twig to start a small blaze; and also one thick length of nearly rotten wood. Propping the flashlight beside him, he heaped the kindling together and rummaged through the bag for matches.

"Quickly!" Jess breathed out.

The leopard reappeared within the beam, much closer, its eyes less opaque, pools of darkness lingering in their lighted depths. It flicked its tail, once, twice, with impatience, its surprisingly small, streamlined head turning away contemptuously as it slunk out of sight.

David glanced up, saw it disappear, and in his haste broke the first two matches. The third flared, and with trembling fingers he set it to the heap of tinder. This immediately caught light and blazed up, sending flickering shadows across the inside of the tree.

"How long will it last?" Jess asked anxiously.

She was still holding the flashlight, her eyes fixed on the pale beam as though she were hypnotized by it. David scooped more of the tinder together and threw another handful into the flames.

"Hard to say," he answered. "A few minutes."

"Is that all?"

"A bit more if we burn the stick."

"What else can we do with it?"

For the second time in as many days she felt close to

tears. The leopard, as if sensing her increased fear, again brushed against the tree, its silky fur sliding along the smooth gray bark. Moments later it skirted the outer circle of light in much the same fashion, grazing the shadowy fringe and melting away, unwilling to approach closer while the fire blazed and crackled within the hollow center of the tree.

David fed the fire steadily, handful by precious handful, the small heap of tinder growing ever smaller. The length of stick still lay alongside the heap, and he kept looking at it, wanting to break it into pieces, but resisting the temptation.

"It's no good staying here until we run out of fuel," he whispered. "We have to get out while we can."

"Get out to where?"

"To the troop. That's where Papio and Upi must have gone."

"But how can we cross all that . . . ? What if . . . ?" She couldn't bring herself to say what was paramount in both their minds.

"There is just one chance—if we take the fire with us."

He felt along the inner edge of the tree trunk and pulled away wisps of dry, stringy moss. More was hanging from the rough wooden walls, blowing gently in the air currents created by the fire. He dragged it down and wound it around the head of the stick, holding it all in place with a narrow strip of cloth ripped from the bottom edge of his shirt.

"A burning torch," he said. "With this and the flashlights, we could keep it off long enough to get there . . . maybe."

97

Jess looked dubiously at the stick in his hand.

"And if it doesn't work?"

"It won't be any worse than staying here."

He threw the last handful onto the fire, waiting for it to die down before he thrust the torch into the dying embers. The dry moss caught instantly, a tight sheath of flame that bit into the rotten timber, igniting it.

"Ready?"

She nodded, standing beside the opening, her flashlight clutched in both hands.

Stepping back, he kicked at the remains of the fire, sending a plume of sparks and hot ashes spinning out into the night. Under cover of that fiery spray, they ducked through the opening and started to run upstream. But after only a few paces David was forced to slow down, the wind threatening to blow the torch out. Walking now, side by side, with the torch held high, they threaded a path through the bush. There was a growl over to their left and Jess shone her flashlight, revealing a shadowy movement in the undergrowth. The same sound, repeated at intervals, swung around behind them and moved up on their other flank. Yet while the torch continued to burn, the leopard came no closer.

As they drew near the stand of fever trees in which the troop was lodged, other sounds disturbed the night— the baboons, terrified of both the strange light and the leopard, hurled abuse at the intruders. At the base of the first tall tree David had to make a decision. Already dark bodies were swarming through the branches above him, screaming out their protests as they fled from the smell and sight of the fire. To have taken the torch any further might have put the whole troop to flight and deprived him and Jess of the communal protection they needed. There was only one thing to do, and swinging the flashlight slowly around, he located the eyes and hurled the torch directly toward them.

Even before it landed, the ember-red tip hissing out its life in the wet grass, he and Jess had slipped away between the tall trunks. Using the flashlights as sparingly as they could, they located a tree whose branches dipped close to the ground and clambered up into it. They were in among the troop now, climbing rapidly from branch to branch, feeling their way up the shadowy trunk. All around them baboons continued to screech and bark, but their cries were directed not at the human intruders: It was the leopard, lurking somewhere within the grove of trees, who was rousing their anger and disapproval.

David reached a fork in the main trunk, wedged himself into it, and pulled Jess up beside him. The noise on every side was deafening, the whole troop voicing its hatred and fear. One dark shape, only feet from where David sat, was shaking branches and roaring for all he was worth. Then, as though some secret signal had been given, the noise stopped abruptly and there was total silence—the kind of eerie, pregnant silence Jess and David had experienced as they had cowered in the hollow trunk of the baobab tree. The night wind sighed through the canopy, rattling the leaves and making the upper branches sway and creak; the constant metallic whir of insects droned on in the background; and the baboons themselves might almost have ceased to exist—the dark figure near to David so still that he merged completely into the shadowy pattern of the night.

The silence stretched on, growing more brittle and frightening with each passing minute. Jess and David, as tense and motionless as the rest of the troop, hardly dared to breath, David's face showing as a pale oval in the darkness. At last, unable to bear the suspense, Jess leaned close to David and whispered, "What's happening?"

His lips brushed her ear, his voice like another breath of wind: "I think the leopard must have climbed into the trees."

His guess soon proved correct. The leopard snarled in the near darkness, and suddenly baboons were leaping through the canopy, furry bodies brushing past David and Jess in their haste to get clear. One young female landed almost on Jess's shoulders and slid down between her knees, resting there a moment, her small body trembling uncontrollably, before she again scampered off.

"David!" Jess broke out, half rising, her scalp prickling with expectation, "it must be . . ."

She never finished. There was an agonized cry, of terror and pain combined, followed by a low purring growl. And after that, silence. Not the deathly hush that had preceded the attack: only the normal quiet and calm of a summer night.

Slowly the baboons moved back to their earlier resting places. Two smaller animals came to the fork where Jess and David still sat and, finding it occupied, climbed out along a nearby limb to another spot close by. Within minutes it was as if the incident had never happened, the whole troop settling to its night's rest. Only the humans continued wide awake, staring into the darkness, both of them too deeply upset to sleep and further burdened by the nagging worry that the fearful scream might have come from either Papio or Upi.

The hours dragged by, punctuated by the occasional cry of an owl or nightjar, or by the faint whisper of bat wings cutting an erratic path above the undulating sea of the canopy. Toward morning one other sound invaded the silence: the regular grumbling and gurgling of the baboons' stomachs as their short muscular bodies objected unmelodiously to the enforced hours of fasting. Under other circumstances Jess would have felt like laughing; but now she took comfort from the homely sound, for it reminded her that she and David were not alone, that there were other warm living creatures all about them.

For the first time in many hours she closed her eyes and relaxed. And the next thing she knew it was morning, the sky bright blue and cloudless above them.

She shook David awake and stretched her arms and legs, trying to ease the ache in her cramped limbs. As far as she could judge, they were in the very center of the troop. Wherever she looked, baboons were rising from their night's rest and moving stiffly along branches. They took little notice of their human companions, even those who were closest to them—the whole troop, as though by mutual consent, accepting these new recruits. Sultan's invisible line, and all the other antagonisms and differences, had been canceled out by their night of shared terror.

In company with the rest, Jess and David climbed slowly down to ground level. To their immense relief Upi and Papio were waiting for them on the forest floor.

"Fine friends you turned out to be," David said, nuzzling Papio playfully, "running off like that and leaving us."

At the sound of his voice, several animals gave them wide berth; and Sultan, watching them narrowly, let out a short, irritable grunt. But it was a warning, a reminder of their tenuous position, not a rejection of them. So that when the troop moved off, David and Jess remained in its midst.

The sun was just rising as they left the cover of the trees, the baboons fanning out across the slope in a broad feeding pattern. David, with the sunlight warm upon his side and back, gave Jess a pleased look.

"They have had it both ways after all," he said.

"Who?"

"Papio and Upi. D'you remember, you said they couldn't have us and the troop too? Well, that's exactly what they do have."

"They do?" she asked inaudibly, the question directed more at herself than at David.

Their slow journey up the slope took them close to the hollow baobab, and David went over and collected the two knapsacks. She waited for him by the stream, watching as white egrets flew overhead in perfect formation. He came and stood beside her, the two of them gazing out over the valley, the whole vast space dotted with formations of birds flying off to their feeding grounds. For as far as they could see there was no smoke, no sign of human habitation to mar the unspoiled beauty of the scene.

"You're not sorry, are you?" he asked quietly.

"About what?"

"About the way things have turned out—us becoming part of the troop."

She was about to make some responsible remark, to warn him that this was only a temporary state of affairs, that with Papio and Upi settled at last there was nothing any longer to keep them there and so they must soon leave. She stopped herself in time, suddenly aware that her immediate feelings had little to do with the future, or even with the past. For the present, she was more than content to stay.

"No, I'm not sorry," she said, and meant it. "This is the best way."

"Really?"

"Yes, really."

And that too was a kind of turning point, a further acceptance on her part of this once alien environment into which they had strayed. It was not that she had so soon forgotten the terrors of the night, or that she clung to a romantic, unreal view of things—after the episode with the leopard and the scream of death in the darkness, that was unthinkable. Clearly, the bush, for all its beauty, contained an element of destruction and harsh necessity. It was this, in a way, which she accepted: the terror not something to be overlooked or ignored, but rather to be seen as a necessary element in the complex world of the escarpment country; a world that had finally reached out and embraced Papio and Upi, using darkness and death to accomplish its purpose.

Even a week earlier, Jess would have regarded such heartless methods as pointless and inhuman, having little to do with her personally. But not any longer. Her encounter with the leopard had merely hastened that process of change that had begun when she had been charged by Sultan. Violence and danger, she now realized deep within herself, were the very conditions of freedom in this place—her own freedom as well as Papio and Upi's. With that realization she moved yet another step closer to the warm, hazardous life of the bush. So that even though her task there was complete, even though common sense prompted her to go home while she had the chance, she found that she had largely lost her desire to leave. As the troop had understood instinctively, she was no longer simply a human being observing them from the outside. Like David, though for different reasons, she was gradually being absorbed into their world; and right at that moment, with the seductive beauty of the valley spread out beneath her, she could see no point in resisting.

Later, she told herself, there would be ample opportunity to break free, to sever these newly formed bonds, later. . . .

NINE

It was a particularly hot afternoon, and the troop, meandering back toward the west, had stopped to rest in one of its favorite places—the giant fig tree where Sultan had once charged at Jess. The scene was much more peaceful now. David was off somewhere, hunting for birds, armed with a weighted throwing stick he had made himself. Jess, less energetic, was lying stretched out on one of the tree's lower limbs.

She felt a slight movement in the branch and Upi came sidling out toward her. Panting slightly from the short climb, she placed four eggs in Jess's hand. Usually, after making one of her gifts, she stayed to be groomed and fondled, but on this occasion she climbed straight back down the tree and approached a nursing mother who was sitting among the buttresslike roots. This female, whom David and Jess knew as Gray because of a whitish patch of fur on her side, had given birth only the night before. The baby, held protectively against its mother's stomach, fascinated Upi, and she kept going back to it, tenderly stroking the black infant fur or brushing her muzzle against the naked pink face. To a lesser degree her fascination was shared by all the animals—so much so that ever since the birth the troop's center of gravity had temporarily shifted from Sultan and the senior males to the nursing mother and her young. Throughout the day they had been the focus of attention. Even Sultan, normally so aloof, had paid ungrudging homage to them.

From her vantage point in the tree, Jess noticed how Gray's many admirers approached almost in a spirit of awe. In itself that made obvious sense, for the ultimate security of the troop depended not only on the stronger males but also on fertile females like Gray, and on the tiny scrap of life she cradled against her. Yet it was more than merely that practical consideration that interested Jess. The regular procession to and fro was also a demonstration of how close-knit the whole troop really was, held together by countless invisible bonds—instinct, affection, kinship, mutual dependence . . . and so the list went on. In short, the troop was a genuine community.

It had taken Jess some time to realize that. During the first day or two she had seen it as little more than a loose collection of animals, all of them more or less alike. After nearly a week in their company, however, she had come to see them very differently. They were actually a miniature society: a society composed of unique individuals, each with his or her own distinct character.

Already many of those characters were familiar to her. Immediately below her now, for instance, lying doglike on the bare sandy soil, was the large senior male who suffered from a skin disorder. Nicknamed Scruffy by David, he had proved to be a gentle creature despite his size and strength. The very young knew from experience that they could romp with him whenever they pleased, his easygoing nature always to be relied upon. In marked contrast was the smaller, broad-shouldered male Jess usually referred to as Muscles. Courageous and aggressive in periods of danger, he was at all other times very nearly intolerable, constantly bickering and fighting with those about them. Once, when Jess had ventured too close, he had turned on her savagely, and only the timely intervention of Sultan had saved her from a nasty mauling. Apart from Sultan, whom he treated with surly respect, he tolerated only three other animals: Ma, an old female who might have been his mother; a much younger female they called Dusty because she was forever on the lookout for dry patches of earth in which to wallow; and Cyclops, a mature male who would have been fairly dominant had he not lost the sight of one eye.

These and other animals Jess had become well acquainted with, and most of them she could recognize even at a distance. But of all the members of the troop, none had impressed her more than Sultan. His very presence gave the troop a sense of security. Even now, while most of the other baboons were sprawled in the shade, he continued to move restlessly among them. In the course of his steady pacing he glanced up and noticed Jess on the branch above him. With a few powerful springs, he was up the tree and stalking out toward her. She waited, and to her surprise he crouched before her and presented himself for grooming.

That gesture in itself was an enormous advance on their early relationship. During her first few days with the troop he regarded her with disdainful tolerance. Only gradually had that attitude broken down. Never before had he allowed himself to be touched by her.

Mindful of the importance of the occasion, she dutifully parted the thick fur, riffling through it with her fingertips. After a while he gave a satisfied grunt and, rising onto his hind legs, made a cursory inspection of her own wild mat of hair. Then, the brief ritual over, he turned and walked away.

The whole encounter could not have lasted more than a few minutes, though that did not blind Jess to its significance. The act of grooming, for any baboon, is a form of intimacy—and it followed that as far as Sultan was concerned, she was now a full member of the troop, with no distinction existing in his mind between her and any other animal in his charge. Curiously, that idea gave her not only pleasure but also a warm feeling of pride, and she was still contemplating that feeling when David appeared at the far edge of the clearing.

As always, Papio was trailing at his heels. Despite his growing attachment to his own kind he could not bear David to go off alone. In all other respects he fitted easily into the life of the troop; his mind seemed to have cleared completely and he was already one of the dominant males. The moment David disappeared, however, he totally lost his newly acquired assurance. Whimpering pitifully, he would look nervously about him and finally go scampering off in pursuit, leaving no doubt at all about where his true allegiance lay.

That same dual response manifested itself now. As they entered the clearing he was following so close on David's heels that he was almost clipping them. A few seconds later, with David safely back within the troop, he turned casually away and went off in search of Upi.

David, seeing Jess lying on the branch, waved a greeting—neither of them raised their voices now because it tended to startle the troop. Climbing easily up into the tree, he came and sat beside her.

"Any luck?" she asked.

He had been keeping one hand out of sight, but now he thrust it forward. Dangling from his fist were three bush doves, their plump gray bodies lifeless and still.

"We eat again," he said.

Taking out his knife, he set about cleaning them, slitting open the stomachs and tossing the contents down to Gray who happily ate up every scrap. That done, he and Jess divided up the eggs, sucking the insides from the shells and swallowing quickly, before they had time to think about the slimy taste.

"Not exactly gourmet cooking," Jess said with a wry smile, "but I guess it has the same effect."

"It must have, because you're looking fine on it."

"A fine mess, you mean!"

They both laughed quietly; but then, suddenly serious, he said:

"Are you satisfied living like this, Jess?"

She could tell from his tone that the question itself was not important—it was only an introduction to something else.

"I'm happy enough," she said, giving him the chance to go on.

He was silent for a few moments, rubbing at the blade of his knife with a bunch of leaves torn from the tree.

"I'm happy here too," he said at last, "but I don't

need to tell you that. What I really want to say is that I . . . I know we can't stay here forever."

"That's true."

"Sooner or later we'll have to give it up. And when the time comes, I will, I promise you that. Even though it'll be hard."

"What'll make it so hard?"

He looked her straight in the face, without any attempt at evasion, all the constraint that had built up between them during their first week in the bush falling away.

"I suppose it's because it's like being part of a huge family here. One that stays together all the time—that doesn't split up. Do you know what I mean?"

"I think so. I see it a bit that way too, except for me it's more like a small village, where everyone depends on everyone else—where nobody's really alone."

"Yes, that's it. Not like home or school. More the way home or school should be."

"All the same, we'll have to leave it some time," she reminded him.

He bent his head over the knife blade, as though concentrating all his attention on the narrow piece of shiny metal.

"That's what I'm getting around to," he said hesitantly. "You see, I don't want to decide about when we should leave. I'd like this to go on for a while longer and then for it just to stop and be over, and for us to be on our way home again."

She looked at him quizzically.

"Are you asking me to decide for you?"

"For both of us."

"Should I let you know in advance?"

He gave the knife an even closer inspection.

"No. Just make up your mind, and when the time comes, tell me. Would you do that?"

She considered the matter for a minute or two. Once, she would have been delighted to receive such a request. Now she wasn't at all sure. After her recent experiences she suspected that for her too it would be far from easy to turn her back on all of this.

"I'd rather we made up our minds together," she admitted.

He shook his head.

"It wouldn't work, not for me. I'd only let you down. It would be different if you fixed it beforehand, though, so I didn't have to think about it. If one day it just happened. I wouldn't let you down then. I wouldn't even argue. All you'd have to do is tell me, say now's the time, and it'd be over. Finished."

Still she hesitated, flinching away from the responsibility he was pushing onto her.

"Perhaps we won't have to make up our minds," she said. "Perhaps in the end everything will be decided for us."

"I don't think that will happen," he answered truthfully.

"No, I guess not. . . ."—and then, reluctantly, "All right, I'll do it. I'll let you know when I think the time's come."

It was easy for her to say the words—but to translate them into action . . . that would be different. Actually to walk away, not only from Papio and Upi, but from the troop, this place, everything. It all sounded so final.

For the moment she shrank from the idea, taking refuge in the reassuring belief that all such decisions could safely be consigned to the future.

As it happened, she was called on to make the first of her decisions that same afternoon.

It was late in the day, long dark shadows reaching across the open ground, the thicker parts of the forest already growing dusky. With the onset of evening the troop was moving slowly up toward a nesting place in the cliffs. Before them lay a narrow gorge between sharp stony ridges, and the baboons entered it fairly tightly bunched, instinctively hurrying as soon as they lost sight of the sun. When they were about halfway along the gorge, effectively hemmed in by the higher ground on either side, they were startled by a rifle shot ahead of them. The whole troop whirled around, frightened but by no means panic-stricken, and began hurrying back over the way they had come, several of the big males deliberately slowing their pace in order to put themselves between the threatened danger and the females and young.

Jess and David, who had been near the rear of the troop, suddenly found themselves leading the retreat. They both broke into a run, with Papio and Upi and some of the larger juveniles loping along beside them. Before they could reach the lower end of the gorge another shot rang out and a man dressed in khaki stepped directly into their path. Had he waited just a few more seconds they would virtually have run into him. As it was, his presence cut off the obvious line of retreat, and now the troop began to panic. Baboons leapt this way and that, screeching in fear, some colliding with each other in the confusion. Above the general uproar the man called out:

"Get down! Both of you!"

He had raised his rifle to his shoulder and Jess realized at once what he intended to do.

"No!" she shouted. "There's no need for that!"

She darted forward and stopped, arms stretched out from her sides, doing her best to block his view. She saw him hesitate, the rifle barrel waver and drop.

It was the delay the troop needed. Following Sultan's example, they were swarming up the western face of the gorge and disappearing over the ridge. Sultan himself was standing on the highest point of the ridge, barking repeatedly, his bulky figure outlined against the flaming sunset.

"Jess!" David called.

She glanced around and saw that he too had climbed halfway up the bank. He called again, and this time there was no mistaking the question in his voice.

"Tell him to come back!" the man ordered her.

Now it was her turn to hesitate, because there were still a few stragglers in the gorge and among them were Papio and Upi. Unlike the rest, they were not trying to scramble free. They had stopped and were looking plaintively from her to David.

"I said to call him back!" the man grated out harshly.

David must have heard him, but he made no response. His eyes were fixed on Jess, waiting for her signal; and when it failed to come—Jess momentarily confused by the unexpectedness of it all—he slithered a few feet down the bank.

Papio's reaction was immediate: With a whimpering grunt, he sprang to David's side, refusing to leave him. Upi was not far behind. Meanwhile, above them Sultan continued to bark, unable to understand why they didn't follow the rest of the troop.

It was his persistent barking that broke through to Jess. In a flash she understood clearly that this was not the way it should end—not like this, with armed men standing over them, threatening Upi and Papio's safety and freedom. The time and the place must be of her choosing, well away from guns and people, just the two of them, sneaking away in the dead of night.

"No!" she called shrilly as David, misinterpreting her silence, slithered the rest of the way down the bank. "Get them both out of here! Quickly!"

She began running up the gorge toward them, mystified by the way he stood there, gazing past her and then, instead of climbing back up the bank, scrabbling in the earth and tufts of grass at his feet.

"Go on!" she shouted.

He straightened up, something in his hand, his arm already drawing back. She looked over her shoulder, saw the man standing with feet wide apart, the rifle to his shoulder—the barrel pointing not at them but toward the ridge where Sultan was still visible. Inwardly she readied herself for the sharp report. Instead, a jagged piece of limestone whizzed past her head and struck the man on the face, slicing his cheek open.

Cursing, he dropped the rifle and clapped both hands to his face. Blood already welled out between his fingers.

"You stupid young fools!" he roared out.

With one bloody hand he was groping for the rifle—while Jess, slipping and sliding on the rocky bank, was hurrying after David and the two baboons. She was the last to reach the top of the ridge. David had already bounded off through the trees; and Sultan, satisfied that she had come to her senses at last, had ducked down out of sight. She didn't follow them right away. From where she was standing she could see the man in the shadowy crevice gap below, one hand clamped over his wounded cheek.

"I'm sorry," she called out, "but I did warn you. There's no need for guns. We're not in any danger."

"You idiot!" he shouted. "Get down here! We've come to protect you, to take you home!"

His voice, she noticed, didn't sound at all protective; it was more threatening and angry.

"We don't need that kind of help," she shouted back, her own anger rising to challenge his. "We'll come out on our own when we're ready. But not if there's any more shooting. Do you understand? You won't get anywhere by using guns."

Turning away, she ran off into the evening, to where Sultan was waiting for her in the cover of the trees.

Had she lingered a few moments longer, she would have heard the man swear quietly to himself and seen how he raised his rifle above his head and shook it ominously at the now empty ridge.

TEN

It was the rain that saved them from immediate pursuit. It fell heavily throughout the night, obliterating any tracks they might have left, and was still drizzling from gray skies when dawn broke. David and Jess, hungry and cold, crept out from the temporary shelter they had made by leaning a few leafy boughs together and capping them with the plastic raincoat. They looked apprehensively at the sodden forest—the trunks of the trees black with rain, the ground saturated and crisscrossed with small rivulets. In the thin light of dawn it was not a welcoming sight, but at least it harbored no immediate danger.

As the light strengthened, the baboons descended from the trees, but they did not then spread out in their usual feeding pattern. The ambush and gunfire had disturbed them deeply, and they now set about putting as much distance as possible between themselves and their pursuers.

Traveling in a southwesterly direction, they followed a curving path that led along the edge of the densely bushed country to the south. Their method of travel surprised Jess and David, who so far had only experienced the relaxed day-to-day wanderings of the troop. Now the baboons were far more purposeful, arranging themselves in a fairly rigid order, like an army on the move. At the front and rear of the troop were the larger juveniles and less dominant males; between these came the low-ranking females and younger juveniles; while in the center of the column were grouped the senior males and the mothers with dependent young. This order not only afforded maximum security for the mothers and young, it also meant that the senior males were always strategically placed. In times of attack they had only to stand still or walk slowly, allowing the endangered part of the column to hurry past.

David and Jess were free to travel in whatever section they preferred; but with their less sensitive eyesight and hearing, they soon realized there was no place for them in the front or rear, and so they took up a position in the center. There they were close to Papio and could see Upi laboring on ahead of them.

It was a long hard day, with the rain falling steadily, matting the coats of the baboons and soaking Jess and David. From time to time the column stopped to feed, but these sessions were always short and the troop soon pushed on again. By early afternoon, exhausted by the constant movement, Upi had slipped back through the ranks of animals and was trailing along at the rear. With an effort she kept her place there for a while, and then, as the strain told, she gradually began to lose contact with the column.

Jess and David had assumed that Sultan would give her time to catch up. But they soon learned one of the harsh realities of baboon life. In times of danger, it is the safety of the whole troop that matters, not that of isolated members. If a single animal falls by the way-side, it is left to fend for itself. So it was with Upi. Sultan barked at her, urging her to keep up; but at no time did he stop the column.

"He's going to leave her behind!" Jess said in a shocked voice.

"We'll see about that," David answered grimly.

He and Jess stopped, allowing the rest of the troop to stream past. Apart from Sultan and Scruffy, and of course Papio who remained at their side, few of the animals spared them a glance, plodding steadily along, their heads lowered against the driving rain. Even the young, riding jockey-style on their mothers' back, took little notice of them, sitting huddled forward clinging to their mothers' wet bodies in order to stay warm.

"What are you going to do?" Jess asked as Upi staggered toward them.

"Carry her."

Handing his knapsack to Jess, he heaved the exhausted Upi onto his back and trudged on. Taking turns, they soon caught up with the troop, and after less than half an hour she was able to walk unaided. But as the afternoon advanced she tired more and more quickly, and they were forced to carry her for longer periods.

When at last the light began to wane they were both in a state of near collapse. Thankfully the rain had stopped, and the sun, just before it set, peeped beneath the cloud cover and sent a few last cheering rays shooting out across the escarpment country, brushing the feathery tops of the trees with gold. That was some consolation to the weary humans. While the troop climbed into a tall cluster of trees they hacked down branches for another of their makeshift shelters and crawled inside. It was over twenty-four hours since they had eaten anything. But after so much rain there was little chance of lighting a fire to cook the birds David had killed on the previous day, and they had no option but to go to bed hungry.

Despite their fatigue, they were too wet and chilled to sleep right away. David was especially restless.

"What's the matter?" Jess whispered.

He shifted uncomfortably on the hard ground.

"It's Upi," he replied. "I keep thinking what would have happened if we hadn't been there today."

"But we were there. Isn't that the important thing?"

"We won't always be, Jess. What then?"

"This kind of situation won't arise very often," she said carefully. "Once we've gone, they'll be left in peace."

He rolled toward her and propped himself up on one elbow.

"You know that isn't true," he said, "so why pretend? Baboons are treated as pests in many parts of the country. They're often hunted and shot at, to stop them from raiding the mealie fields and to keep their numbers down. Scenes like last night and today are going to happen whether we're here or not. Sooner or later Upi will be abandoned."

"Yes, but not for long," she assured him. "She'll catch up again. She's no fool—she knows how to follow a trail. At worst she'll spend a night or two alone in the bush."

"That's what I keep thinking about: her being on her own. After what she's been through already, it doesn't seem fair."

She reached up through the darkness and touched his

face, his skin damp in the moist night air.

"There's nothing fair about this place, David, any more than there was about the research center. But at least the bush is where she belongs. It's hers in a way those cages could never have been. Even if she does spend nights alone, isn't that better than having her back inside the enclosure?"

"I wouldn't wish that on her," he murmured unhappily.

"Anyway," she added, "you're assuming Papio won't stay with her. I'm not at all sure about that. When it comes down to it, he'll probably choose Upi rather than the troop."

There was a rustle of leaves as he lay down again.

"Yes, I suppose you're right," he said softly, partly reassured. "There's always Papio. . . . Papio will watch out for her."

His voice sounded suddenly drowsy and within moments he was asleep. Yet even though her whole body ached with weariness, she remained awake for some time. She had understood, without needing to ask, what lay behind David's anxiety: not just a vague fear for Upi's safety, but more precisely the prospect of their having to abandon both her and Papio. It was very much her own anxiety too. Ever since the ambush, she had known that that was the only way—for them both to creep off under cover of night. Papio's deep attachment to David ruled out any other possibility. It would have to be done secretly, without endearments or farewells. So why not now? At this moment? She half rose . . . and sank back again. They were both too tired. Just the same, it had to be soon. The question was—when?

There in the stillness of the night, with David breathing deeply and evenly beside her, she faced that question squarely for the first time—and immediately saw a way out of her dilemma. She would allow the baboons to decide for her. She and David would stay with the troop as long as it followed a westerly course, for that was the direction they had to take in order to reach the escarpment road. Then, when the troop turned back toward the east, they would sneak off, make a quick dash for the road.

Yes, that was the best plan. It meant that she, like David, could take each day as it came. Also, it guaranteed a little more time with the troop, perhaps as much as a week. What harm could that do? Hadn't she shouted at the man—no more guns, no more shooting? He had heard her, she was certain of that. And he would surely do as she asked. Or would he? A germ of doubt entered her mind and was quickly put aside. She was too tired to consider what might happen if . . . No, the man would leave them alone for the time being. He *had* to. Meanwhile, the baboons' lives would continue undisturbed, even though, without realizing it, they would be the ones making the final choice.

There was, Jess felt, a certain rightness about that. The troop, which had freely taken them into its protection, would also decide when they should leave—animals temporarily ordering the affairs of humanity. With that thought, content at last, she snuggled against David and gave herself up to sleep.

The following morning completely matched Jess's new lightness of mood. The sun rose into a clear sky, the bush awoke from its rain-soaked stupor—and the troop had lost the sense of urgency that had driven it throughout the previous day. Long before the sun was showing above the treetops, the baboons had spread out across the slope and begun to feed. From then until dusk they traveled barely two miles, all their energy directed toward the search for food.

Throughout that long, uneventful day David and Jess also spent their time hunting for things to eat. The three carcasses they had brought with them had unfortunately gone bad; but as David demonstrated, it was not difficult to replace them, though it took time and patience. He would listen for the call of a bush dove, and then, armed with a short, sturdy stick, he would creep toward it, answering the bird's call as he went. It was an easy sound to mimic, and the bird, fascinated by the familiar cry, would either remain where it was, allowing him to approach to within a few yards, or actually fly toward him and perch on a nearby tree. At such close range he usually scored a hit—and the heavy stick, although a crude weapon, was a merciful and effective one.

It was not a task that David enjoyed, though it was necessary to their survival; and by midday, with six gray feathered bodies hanging from his belt, he was glad enough to stop. Returning to the troop, he found that Jess had also been successful. As well as collecting eggs and fledglings, she had managed to catch a number of lizards. The lizards looked especially unappetizing, but roasted over hot coals they smelled and tasted as good as any other meat, as she and David had discovered some days earlier.

Altogether, their morning's hunting had not yielded a great deal, but it was enough for their immediate needs, and withdrawing a reasonable distance from the troop, they cooked and ate their first meal in nearly two days.

Their hunger temporarily satisfied, they spent the hot part of the afternoon with the troop, David sleeping in the deep shade and Jess watching the young baboons romping together. What interested her was not just the young and their antics but also Upi, the way she hovered around them with motherly concern, always ready to comfort the distressed. It was possible that because of her weakened condition she would never bear offspring, yet her maternal instincts were fully awakened and now she rarely wandered far from the young.

Jess, too, fell into a doze eventually. But as soon as the shadows began to lengthen, she and David resumed their search for food. This time they were less fortunate. There were far fewer bush doves in the vicinity, and Jess wasted what remained of the afternoon trying to catch the large blue-headed lizards that fed on the forest floor. No matter how cautiously she approached, they always spotted her and scrambled up the nearest tree, taking care to keep the bulk of the trunk between themselves and her. With repeated failures, it began to look as though she and David would go to sleep hungry that night. Then, just as the evening was drawing close, they had a stroke of good fortune.

The troop had chosen for its nightly resting place a growth of low but dense bush. As they approached it, they encountered a flock of guinea fowl that was obviously intent on roosting nearby. Normally the birds would have run off at the first sight of human beings, but the fact that the troop was calm reassured them slightly, because after milling around for a few moments they took quietly to the trees, calling softly to each other through the twilight. David and Jess gave them time to settle; then, as darkness descended, they crept in under the roosting birds. From that point on their task was simple. Jess, shining a flashlight up into the darkness, transfixed one of the birds while David dispatched it quickly and cleanly with his throwing stick. The others, roused by the noise and light, stirred uneasily. Like the baboons however, they were scared of the dark and preferred to remain where they were, seeking safety in absolute stillness—their speckled feathers puffed up around them, their small heads, tipped with white and red, tucked in between their wings. In that position they were sitting targets, and David could have killed any number; but he took only what they needed, and when three lifeless bodies were lying on the leaf-strewn ground they left the remaining birds in peace.

Later that night, sitting beside a banked-up fire, Jess and David felt more satisfied than they had for days. They had eaten the biggest of the three guinea fowls—a bird considerably larger than the average chicken—and were busy roasting the other two for food on the following day. Jess, feeling unusually lazy and contented, watched while David pushed one of the clay-wrapped carcasses deeper into the coals. In the yellowish light of the flames she could see just how dirty and disheveled he looked: his shirt and jeans so ragged and torn that they barely covered him; his hair a wild and knotty mess; his face darkened as much by woodsmoke and dirt as by constant exposure to the sun. She knew that she must look just as bad, but none of that seemed to matter anymore. It was all somehow irrelevant. The only really important thing was her present feeling of well-being—that, and the knowledge that Papio and Upi and the rest of the troop were sleeping safely in the treetops nearby.

"Isn't it strange how things turn out," she said dreamily. "A month ago we were both living in houses, and food was something that came out of shops. I didn't even want to think about things being killed for food then. Yet here we are, only weeks later, existing like a couple of primitive hunters."

David rocked back onto his heels, flicking at the ashes with a piece of twig.

"Yes, we've become a little like the animals we're trying to save. Still, there's nothing wrong with that. Nor with this," he added, poking at the carcass in the fire. "Everything has to live by killing something else. It's the way things are. What I can't stand is useless killing—killing for its own sake. It's not only cruel— there's no point to it."

He had grown suddenly serious, and Jess guessed what he was referring to—the fate that awaited so many of the animals in the enclosure.

"At least we've saved Papio and Upi from that," she replied—and had a sudden disquieting vision of the man, gun in hand, who had ambushed them in the gorge. Hastily, as she had once before, she banished the image, choosing not to think about it—not now, in the placid stillness of the night. "Whatever else happens to them," she went on, clinging stubbornly to her present sense of well-being, "here in the bush they'll never again be exposed to that sort of pointless cruelty."

Soon afterward she and David lay down close to the

fire and went to sleep. Yet not many hours later Jess had cause to remember those last words of hers, recalling them with a bitterness so intense that it came close to poisoning the even flow of her young life.

ELEVEN

The water hole was located in a shallow basin between two ridges, where a stream was partially dammed by a tumble of boulders and an accumulation of silt and debris. Immediately around the pool there was little growth, the sandy shoreline a bare whitish-yellow in the sunlight. Beyond this shoreline, the bush stood like a dense green wall, a tangle of trees and shrubs that flourished on the seepage from the stream. It was within this fringe that the female duiker, a tiny antelope not much bigger than a terrier, was cowering.

The troop came upon her as they approached the pool from below. She moved gingerly out of their way, content to let them precede her. She seemed more cautious than alarmed, her pointed nose constantly testing the air. As they passed her, her whole body twitched nervously and she slid away through the undergrowth.

Her reaction was not in itself surprising; there was nothing unusual about animals taking fright at their first glimpse of humans. Even so, Sultan halted immediately, and Muscles followed suit, peering about them with distrust.

Under other circumstances the troop might have taken

their hesitation for a warning and crept away. The afternoon was hot, however, and this was the only water they had encountered since early morning. Also, at the front of the troop, leading the way, was a group of senior adults—among them, Ma, Cyclops, and Gray—and seeing them push eagerly forward, many of the others followed.

David and Jess, lacking the keen communal awareness of the troop, were not even conscious that anything was amiss. Their first inkling of any restiveness occurred when Papio let out a soft breathy grunt. They had by then reached the edge of the thick bush and could see the pool and its sandy border through a thin veil of leaves. Already a number of baboons were picking their way across the sand and stooping at the water's edge—all of which made Papio's warning appear somewhat odd. Nonetheless, mindful of his sharper sight and hearing, they both stopped.

"What is it, boy?" David murmured.

Papio's mantle had lifted and he was standing thrust forward, most of his weight resting on his hands. Again he grunted, the sound so soft and low it was hardly audible. It was echoed by Sultan who had sidled up alongside him, the two animals standing almost with shoulders touching, listening intently. Like the duiker, they appeared not so much alarmed as ill at ease.

David and Jess strained their ears for the slightest sound. They could hear nothing save the cicada-heavy silence—though they noticed how the baboons who had already ventured into the open suddenly lifted their heads or paused in their progress across the sand. A moment later there was a tremor of movement high above them.

Looking up, they saw a group of vervet monkeys clustered together on a limb that thrust out over the pool, their light-gray bodies only just visible against the sun-washed blue of the sky. One of the monkeys detached itself from the rest and ran farther out along the limb. With arms and legs stretched wide, he pushed his small head forward, intent on something below. Whatever he was looking for must have moved or shown itself at that point, because with a screech he scurried back along the limb.

What happened next occupied the space of only a few seconds, yet that in no way diminished its lasting importance for David or Jess. The baboons at the water's edge glanced up with startled faces, their eyebrows raised, water dripping from their muzzles. Then Sultan and Papio leapt out into the open, Sultan giving his short, explosive bark that always signaled a general alarm. David and Jess, concerned for Papio's safety, made the fatal error of following him. No sooner had they stepped clear of the bush than a voice rang out:

"Yes, this is the one."

Almost simultaneously they saw them: three men, dressed in khaki, moving quickly out of the bush on the far side of the pool, their rifles already to their shoulders. There were several loud reports, coming close upon each other, and three baboons, all well clear of the humans, reeled and fell. One was a young male who toppled silently into the pool, a red stain billowing cloudlike into the water around him. Another was a mature female with a young child—she half turned, pawed ineffectually at the wet sand, and lurched sideways, her tiny baby being flung clear as her dead body rolled down the shelving bank. The third animal hit was Sultan. The impact jerked him backward but failed to kill him. Grunting and coughing, he rose onto all fours and dragged himself back into the cover of the bush.

All the remaining baboons, except for one, were scrambling for safety—and that one was Upi. Bounding toward the pool, she slithered to a halt beside the orphaned baby, gathered it up with one hand, and holding the small body tightly against her scarred breast, leapt after the retreating troop.

It was all over so quickly that only Jess and David were left standing on the bare sand. On the far side of the pool the men were reloading, the bolts of their rifles clicking viciously in the silence, though there was nothing now for them to aim at. They stood in a straight line, surveying their handiwork, the central member of the trio slightly in advance of the other two. He was a tall, heavily built man with a large, reddish-brown bandage covering most of his left cheek, and it was at him that Jess and David were staring.

"I told you . . . !" Jess said in a shocked, choked voice. "I told you . . . !"

But she could not find words to express her feelings of outrage and dismay. Bending down, she scooped up fistfuls of sand and flung them at the hated figure—the fine particles, caught by the light breeze, floating out across the pool and settling gently, almost soothingly, on the two bloody bodies that wallowed in the shallows.

"Come on, Jess!" David urged her, tugging at her arm. "We can't do anything here!"

Even through the fog of rage and pain she knew he

130

was right—the man, the Hunter, had a gun, while they had only their bare hands. Their only possible recourse was escape.

"This is the end of your little jaunt," the Hunter called out. "Stand exactly where you are until we get there."

But whereas he had to skirt the wide pool, David and Jess had only to step back through the dense wall of bush. Before the men could cover a fraction of the distance, David had dragged Jess out of sight.

For the first forty or fifty yards she allowed herself to be pulled along, still too shocked to take stock of the situation. Without David's encouragement she might even have given up. Her arms and legs felt strangely heavy, as though she had been drugged, and all she really wanted was to lie down in the shade and forget everything that had happened, to resign herself to the oblivion of sleep. That feeling did not last long, for directly in their path was Sultan.

Unable to keep up with the rest of the troop, he had fallen far behind, crawling as best he could through the undergrowth. Now he was quite still, his head lowered, his back curved with pain. At the sight of him, all Jess's lethargy vanished. With a cry of concern, she darted forward and would have gone to him had David not held her back.

"No, leave him!" he warned.

He was not being callous, nor merely expressing the law of the troop, which ordained that only the strong should survive. More than anything else he was aware of the peril of the situation—the peril to Jess. But careless of her own safety, she shrugged him off and knelt beside the stricken leader.

The bullet had hit him in the right lung, and his short

painful breaths were rasping and gurgling in his throat. He seemed on the brink of death, lacking even the strength to hold up his head. Yet as soon as Jess touched him, he somehow found the energy to turn on her, his powerful jaws clamping onto her forearm. Had he wanted to, he could have broken her arm with a single crunching bite, but he chose not to. In spite of the pain that clutched him, he still saw her as part of the troop, as a creature to be protected. And after mouthing her arm for a second or two, he released her, his head drooping forward once again.

"Come, Sultan," Jess murmured soothingly.

Slipping her head under his arm, she eased him upright. He tried to help her, coughing with the effort, sending a spray of blood over her face and hair. She hardly noticed it, all her attention fixed on the problem of getting Sultan to some place of sanctuary. To her left, she could hear the men crashing through the bush in pursuit of the troop. That at least gave them a period of respite, and she knew they dared not waste it.

"David!" she pleaded desperately.

He was already lifting Sultan's other shoulder, the two of them half-dragging, half-leading the heavy animal through the maze of trees and leafy bushes.

"Which way?" Jess gasped out.

He nodded to the right, and between them they managed to haul Sultan as far as the stream. There, waiting for them, was Papio, who seemed to have realized which direction they must take. As on an earlier occasion, they hung the knapsacks around his neck and again lifted Sultan, staggering downstream, keeping as far as possible to the rocky part of the bed.

The next hour was a grueling time for both of them. They seldom spoke—Jess, especially, tight-lipped and silent—and they rested only when one of them literally slumped down with exhaustion. It was much worse for Sultan. Again and again he choked on the blood welling up in his throat, coughing out his own precious life in a fine crimson spray that dried and caked on their skin and tattered clothing.

"It's no good," David said finally, stumbling to a halt.

Jess stopped without a word. Sultan had reached the stage where he could no longer bear his own weight; he was sagging between them, his head fallen sideways. With his tongue lolling from his mouth and his eyes rolled right back, he appeared more dead than alive, his breath coming in feeble, bubbling gasps. They laid him on the bank and watched helplessly as his panting grew more rapid and erratic, blood dripping from his tongue and trickling down through the fur on his chest.

"He's nearly gone," David said quietly.

Again Jess didn't answer, standing perfectly still, her face expressionless. There was nothing she or David could do. The fierce head jerked back. The snorting, strangled breathing rasped out for the last time, and then the whole body sagged into an attitude of deep rest.

David wiped the sweat wearily from his forehead.

"Thank God that's over," he said.

Crouching down, he closed the sightless eyes and eased the gaping jaws together. Jess, standing beside him, continued to watch wordlessly, her eyes fixed on the still form. He gave her a few minutes to collect herself, one arm held protectively about her shoulders.

"Let's leave him now, Jess," he said softly.

She refused to move, pushing him off with an abrupt gesture. When he took her hand and tried to draw her away, she rounded on him angrily, grabbing him by the shirt collar and shaking him violently to and fro.

He didn't resist, allowing her to work out her pent-up emotion, readying himself for that moment when, panting like a cornered animal, she gave up the struggle and sagged against him, her face half-buried in the hollow of his neck.

Beside them, Papio grunted once, registering his concern at their behavior, but David silenced him with a movement of the hand.

"I should have guessed something like this would happen," Jess whispered hoarsely, an oddly stricken quality to her voice. "The man in the gorge. The Hunter! I knew we shouldn't have trusted him. And yet . . . and yet . . ."

"Hush, now," David answered. "You have nothing to blame yourself for."

"Don't I?" It was more of an appeal than a question.

"You didn't cause any of this, Jess," he said reassuringly. "It was *him, his* doing. Not ours."

His words seemed to steady her because she pulled free and stood facing him, dry-eyed and strangely implacable. All the gentleness had drained from her features, her profound sense of hurt transforming her into another person, one he barely recognized.

"You're right!" she said fiercely, convinced now, holding out her blood-spattered arms. "All of this, it's on his hands now! His! Because I told him, the Hunter, that we didn't want the guns. The night of the ambush. And he heard. Yet he still went ahead and did it. This!"

She brandished her fists like weapons, a fanatical glint in her eyes. "He's the one to blame now. Him! And all the rest!"

"The rest?"

"The ones who sent him! Anyone who let him do these things!"

David was vaguely conscious of having said something like that himself once, prior to their raid on the mealie field. He too had been ready to see everyone as an enemy. Yet those same sentiments expressed by Jess sounded so much more extreme, and he was momentarily taken aback.

"Hold on," he said cautiously, "maybe some of them . . ."

But Jess, too deeply moved by grief and pain, had passed the point where she could think clearly, her rational nature smothered by a growing sense of outrage.

"No, they're all to blame! All of them!" she insisted adamantly.

Instead of replying, he took the two knapsacks from Papio and shouldered them both. When he turned back toward her he looked different, as though in those few moments he had begun to mature. There was in his face little of that childish, dependent quality that had so alarmed Jess weeks earlier.

"Maybe . . . maybe we should think about going home," he said hesitantly.

It wasn't what he really wanted to do. The suggestion came from him almost involuntarily, prompted by a feeling of uneasiness.

"How can you talk about home at a time like this!" she said hotly.

"But you said . . ."

"That was before . . . before they killed Sultan."

"It wasn't our families who did that, Jess."

"Yes, it was them too," she said, and began to cry, bitter hurtful tears that did nothing to ease her distress. "They let it happen, didn't they? They could have stopped it."

David shuffled his feet uncomfortably, unsure of how to answer her.

"I still think we should make plans . . . I mean about going home," he said, though speaking with the same uncertainty as before, not yet ready within himself to leave Papio.

Jess dashed the tears angrily from her eyes, as though she resented them, saw them as an unwelcome sign of weakness.

"That isn't for you to decide," she reminded him sharply, her voice suddenly cold and decisive. "We have an agreement, remember?"

"But we made the agreement before we even knew about the Hunter."

"It makes no difference. You promised. You said you'd go along with whatever I decided."

He nodded, not seriously wanting to oppose her.

"All right," he said, "we'll keep to that. If that's what you want—if you think it's best."

She responded by stripping off her ragged shirt and draping it carefully over Sultan's damaged body, like a shroud.

"What are you doing?" he asked, his voice grown quiet.

"I'm deciding," she said, smoothing out the cloth with loving care.

"Deciding?"

"Yes, that we aren't going back out there."

He crouched beside her, feeling an odd mixture of discomfort and relief.

"You mean never?"

But she was too distraught to think beyond the present. The fact of Sultan's cruel and unnecessary death crowded out every other consideration, her normally clear mind clouded and confused. She looked again at the dead body at her feet, the once powerful limbs strangely pathetic in the attitude of death.

"Not out there," she repeated doggedly, beginning to cry again, her tears falling on to the soft gray-brown fur, "not now, not after this."

TWELVE

They soon discovered that the troop had reverted to its former tactic of skirting the thickly forested region further down the slope, heading back toward the east. Jess and David knew that country well by now, and with Papio leading they hurried after the fleeing baboons.

As they had expected, they came upon Upi first, at about noon on the following day. Burdened with the extra weight of the infant, she had fallen behind even more quickly than before, and when they found her she was lying exhausted in the shade of a tall seringa tree. She whimpered softly when she saw them, clutching at the small pink-faced baby for fear they might take it from her.

"It's all right, Upi," Jess murmured, fondling the soft fur beneath her chin, "we'll have you back with the others soon."

That was no idle promise, for they had already worked out a plan of action. While David cut young branches, Jess twisted strands of long-stemmed grass into makeshift ropes, and from these simple materials they quickly fashioned a crude litter. Within an hour they were on their way again, Upi and the baby cradled comfortably between them.

That day, sustained only by the remains of the last guinea fowl, they pressed on steadily. Not until the stars were showing overhead did they stop, and they were up again before dawn, moving off as the first trace of gray brushed the sky. Their haste was soon rewarded, for shortly before noon they came upon the troop.

It was clear that the Hunter had not disturbed them since the ambush beside the pool because they were spread out over a wide area, foraging peacefully. They showed no alarm at the arrival of the newcomers, but Scruffy and Muscles, who now appeared to be sharing the leadership, came stalking over with the obvious intention of establishing their new authority. They sniffed only briefly at the humans, their attention centered on Papio. Muscles was the first to stop before him and present himself for grooming.

It was, as Jess and David knew full well, an act of dominance, much in the same way as Papio's compliance would have been an act of submission. But this too, like Upi's exhaustion and abandonment, they were both expecting and prepared for.

"No, Papio!" David said sternly.

Startled, Papio glanced toward him, trying to figure out what he was supposed to do.

"I said no!" David grated out.

Aware only that something unusual was happening, Papio made no move to groom the proffered back. And Muscles, always quick to anger, puffed out his mane and turned threateningly toward him. That was when David issued his second command.

"Here, boy!" he ordered, and gestured for Papio to ignore Muscles and come crouch at his heels.

It was a calculated move, not without some danger

to David himself. For Muscles, angered beyond endurance by this open flouting of his authority, shifted his attention to David, charging straight toward him. It was what Jess and David had thought he might do, and it was also his mistake. There was a roar from Papio, a blur of two bodies colliding, and the next moment Muscles was rolling over on the ground. He was up in an instant, by no means ready to submit. As he slowly advanced on this new challenger, so too did Scruffy.

Again David was prepared. In between carrying the litter, he had busied himself fashioning a cudgel for this kind of encounter. Now he put it to good use, swinging the heavy-ended stick straight at Scruffy—catching him by surprise and making him leap back out of range. It was all the opportunity Papio needed. Using his superior weight and speed, he thrust in against Muscles, grasping him by the throat and shaking him vigorously before casting him aside and turning on his other attacker. Scruffy was almost equal to Papio in size and strength, yet he lacked the aggressive drive of a true leader, and he gave in without a struggle, cowering doglike, his lips drawn back in a nervous grimace.

Jess, who had been standing to one side, looking on, let out a deep sigh.

"He's done it," she said thankfully.

"I don't think so," David answered. "If you ask me, it's only the first round."

That was in fact the case. In the course of the afternoon Muscles made two further attempts to reassert his authority. The first resulted in little more than a skirmish, but the final encounter was decisive. With a deep gash on his shoulder, Muscles gave up any lingering claims to leadership. Cowering on the ground, his face turned aside, he made no protest as Papio stood threateningly above him. And when Papio presented himself for grooming he obediently picked through the still bristling fur of the new leader.

That night, sitting cozily within the circle of firelight, Jess and David had some reason to be pleased. Equally, they knew well enough that they were only halfway toward achieving their aim of securing both themselves and the troop against the Hunter.

"Do you think they'll follow Papio anywhere now that he's leader?" Jess asked, for that was the real issue.

She was lying on her back, staring up at the stars that showed through a gap in the trees. The tiny, brilliant points of light seemed to waver and shift within the heated currents of air rising from the fire, creating the impression that this spot where she and David lay was somehow the pivotal point upon which the vast reaches of the universe depended and moved.

"It's hard to say," he answered. "Baboons have a strong territorial sense. This troop's territory, judging by the way they've acted so far, is confined to the upper part of the escarpment. It may be pretty tough getting them to move elsewhere."

"Even with Papio leading them?"

"Leaders can be challenged. We saw that today. If he pushes them too hard, they may gang up on him. That's the way things work within a troop. A sort of mixture between dictatorship and democracy—one system modifying the other."

Jess rolled over onto her stomach, her face cradled thoughtfully in both hands.

"All right," she said, "then we'll just have to support

him. We'll be the ones who do the ganging up."

She spoke with a grim determination that had come to characterize so many of her utterances since the death of Sultan.

"It might work," David replied.

"It has to. Somehow or other we have to get the troop to move further south. The only place we'll all be safe is deeper in the valley. It's a vast area, covered in thick bush. We'll have a real chance against the Hunter there."

David didn't question her reference to the Hunter—not because he had forgotten about the other men who had fired on the troop, but because in the minds of both him and Jess, the Hunter, the man with the cut cheek, now symbolized everything they were trying to escape from, the world that they had come to think of as "out there," an alien region they instinctively avoided.

"I just wish we could explain about the Hunter to the troop," he said wistfully. "It would all be so much easier."

"There's no easy way out of this now," she replied shortly. "All we can do is back Papio up."

And she reached out and selected one of the heavy sticks they had brought for the fire, testing its weight in her right hand.

Despite their apprehensions, the next day began well. At dawn, David, with Papio at his heels, had no difficulty in persuading the troop to head south. Now fully rested after their flight from the Hunter, they ambled easily along, stopping frequently to browse or search for grubs and other insects among the fallen leaves. For a while it seemed that David and Jess's task was going to be easy—that their fears concerning the troop's territorial sense were ill-founded. But by slow degrees a certain uneasiness made itself felt; and soon some of the mature animals began to show a reluctance to journey further down the slope. They constantly veered off to the left or right, only returning to the main body of the troop when Papio barked out a recall.

Not surprisingly, the first animal to be openly defiant was Muscles. Surrounded by a group of juveniles, he ignored Papio's summoning barks, and David and Papio had to set off after him.

That particular rebellion was soon quelled. Papio swept imperiously through the small group, nipping some, shoulder-charging others, and turning on Muscles with a display of savagery that reduced him instantly to a state of submission.

Any feeling of victory was short-lived, however. The atmosphere in the troop was electric, the widespread tension manifesting itself in a number of ways. Animals began squabbling over insignificant morsels of food; others quarreled and slashed at each other for no observable reason; and the young remained close to their mothers, acting exactly as if the troop were threatened.

As David and Jess guessed it would, the tension finally erupted into an open confrontation. This time the rebellious faction was led not by Muscles but by Gray. As a senior female and a mother nursing the most recently born child, she was one of the highest ranking animals in the troop. Flanked by Scruffy and Cyclops, and supported by several lowlier animals, she stalked resolutely toward Papio.

"This is it!" Jess murmured.

With a heavy stick gripped tightly in both hands, she moved to Papio's side. David was already in position, the three of them unmoving as the opposing group advanced.

What followed was almost like a performance of mime. While the children looked on, unsure of what to expect, the animals went through a series of threatening gestures: some yawning or flattening their ears, others grinding their teeth or raising and lowering their brows. To an outsider it might all have appeared vaguely comic. To David and Jess, caught up in the tension of the moment, it was a matter of deadly seriousness, for they knew that these were just the preliminaries.

It was Gray who showed the first signs of real aggression. Darting forward with lightning speed, she swiped at Papio and hastily withdrew. He retaliated by rearing up on his hind legs and roaring out a challenge, while David and Jess lifted their clubs in readiness. Before any of them could make another move, a third and totally unexpected element entered the drama. Upi, temporarily abandoning her adopted child, leapt in from behind and gave Gray a sharp nip on the nape of the neck. Confused at being threatened from two sides, Gray whirled around; and Papio, seizing the opportunity, shoulder-charged Scruffy, sending him crashing into the animals immediately behind. There was a brief period of total confusion—some baboons leaping aside, others standing with hackles raised, unsure of whether to advance or retreat—and for a few seconds Jess feared there was going to be a free-for-all.

What averted it was as unexpected as Upi's attack on Gray: a simple action that was itself a complete testimony to the troop's ability to survive as a community and not destroy itself with internal dissension. For while all the other animals were glaring or snarling at each other, Ma, the eldest and in some ways the most respected of the females, suddenly abandoned the conflict altogether. As calm and unhurried as ever, she picked her way carefully between the combatants and walked off down the slope. The effect of her action was to defuse the situation completely. The anger and excitement ebbed away as every head turned to watch her go: a stiff-jointed, bowed figure setting out alone for the depths of the valley.

There was no overall move to follow her example— not to begin with. Then gradually, one by one, other baboons began to turn their backs on the conflict and set out after her. Until at last there was a general exodus, with even Gray gathering up her tiny baby and trotting off with the rest.

Jess and David, relieved beyond measure, lowered their clubs and smiled at each other.

"They really had me worried for a minute," Jess admitted.

"Me too. But we should have guessed Papio and Upi wouldn't let us down. They were both fantastic."

"And Ma. Don't forget her."

"Yes, we're becoming a regular pair of animal trainers. At this rate we could join a circus."

Jess frowned and looked at him disapprovingly.

"All right," he added quickly, grinning at her, "only joking."

"I know, but it didn't sound right. After all, we're not changing their territory for our sake—only for theirs.

Now that Sultan's gone, we're the ones who have to look after them."

"What about Papio? We couldn't do anything without him."

"Yes, that's what I mean really: us and Papio. Together, we'll soon have them settled and happy again."

That was not to be so easily accomplished. The old habits of the troop could not be eradicated by a single encounter. Although the baboons had consented to leave their former territory, they were by no means happy about the change. Throughout the afternoon they kept close together and were much more jittery and nervous than usual. If Papio relaxed his vigilance for a moment, one or two groups, under the guise of foraging, would wander back toward the north.

Using a mixture of patience and bullying, Jess and David managed to coax them on, and by evening they had penetrated the thick growth deep in the valley. That night they nested in a group of fever trees that were taller and more luxuriant than any they had known in the high country. Yet the added security did little to comfort them. They remained restive for an hour or more after dark, grunting and calling to each other, their uneasy murmurs persisting throughout the night.

Nor were they any better on the following day. The strange surroundings, the lack of any recognizable landmarks, continued to disturb them, and they were quick to take fright. A small event, like the discovery of a scorpion, which usually alarmed only the animals in the immediate vicinity, was now sufficient to send the whole troop leaping away in a state of panic.

Virtually the only one who seemed content was Upi.

With Jess and David nearby and her newly acquired baby either clutched to her breast or riding jockey-style on her back, she had all that she really desired. Upi's contentment, however, was not enough to compensate for the general air of unhappiness that permeated the troop, and that afternoon, during the long rest period, David expressed vague misgivings.

"Perhaps we're asking too much of them," he said uncertainly. "It might have been better to move them in easy stages—by taking them out of their territory a few hours at a time."

But Jess was adamant, the image of Sultan's terrible death still strong upon her, her sense of outrage still obscuring everything but her fixed determination to oppose the Hunter.

"No, this is the best way," she said firmly. "After a while they'll get used to it. You'll see."

"What if they don't?"

"They'll just have to," she answered, her voice hard and inflexible. "It's their safety that comes first, not their happiness."

"Their safety?" David replied uneasily, a sudden disturbing thought crossing his mind. "But aren't we . . . ?"

Quickly, he suppressed the idea, not even wanting to consider the unpleasant likelihood that perhaps it was their presence, his and Jess's, that was now endangering the troop. Jess just as quickly supported him, her present state of mind making it impossible for her to place the blame anywhere but at the feet of the men with the guns.

"No!" she said, her anger, never far from the surface

147

now, flaring up again. "It's the Hunter who's threatening them. Him and his kind. We're here to protect them."

"Yes . . ." David agreed, and then more confidently, "yes."

They were still speaking in much the same vein when, two days later, they first heard the dog.

THIRTEEN

They saw the dog before it saw them. It was a thin hoop-backed animal from one of the villages, nosing its way along the very game trail the troop had taken that morning. From their hiding place amid the thick foliage, Jess and David watched it draw closer. For both of them an eerie quality had crept into the afternoon, because they suspected the dog was walking toward its own death—Papio, crouched tensely beside them, waiting only for that critical moment when he would lunge forward.

Luckily for the dog, it detected their presence in time. A sudden eddy of wind warned it of imminent danger, and it leapt aside just as Papio charged from cover. Yelping with fright, its tail tucked so far between its legs that the tip curled against its stomach, it pelted off down the path—only to crash into the legs of its oncoming master.

They both recognized him at once. Not the Hunter, as they had feared, but the boy from the village—the same soft, intelligent eyes, the same unaggressive face and manner. And they stepped out to meet him.

Suddenly confronted by them, he paused in mid stride,

a look of surprise, almost of shock, on his face. Jess guessed that it wasn't just the unexpectedness of the meeting that he found so astonishing, but rather the marked change in their appearance. In a flash of insight, she saw how they must really look to him: more like two wild creatures than human beings. She herself half naked, both of them dirty and bedraggled, and with a new furtiveness about the way they moved, a foreign, untrusting quality apparent in their eyes.

All of this he must have taken in with a single glance, because his surprise was only momentary, and then his natural politeness took over. Smiling in a friendly way, he advanced to meet them, while Papio, disturbed by this unwanted intruder, grunted a warning.

"Steady," David murmured.

The boy, seemingly untroubled by Papio's nearness, stopped a few feet away and placed a bundle of mealies on the ground between them.

"I am bringing present," he said in his faltering English.

David made as if to kick it aside, contemptuously, but Jess, remembering how the boy had helped her, drew David back. Picking the bundle up by the loop of the string that bound it, she said:

"Thank you for the food. But why have you followed us?"

"I am coming here . . ." he began, and stopped as he noticed Papio sidling around to where the dog was crouched behind him.

"I think we'd better keep these two apart," Jess said. "Look, tie your dog up and we'll go off somewhere and talk."

She touched Papio's shoulder and pointed back along the trail, and reluctantly he walked off, returning to the frightened troop. The boy, meanwhile, muttered a few words in Nyanja, and the dog obediently lay down.

"That's better," Jess said, and with the other two following her, she led the way down to a nearby watercourse.

Higher up the escarpment it would have been no more than a rivulet, but here, so much closer to the Zambezi, it had broadened out into a winding stream. It was bordered by gently sloping banks of sand on which wagtail birds strutted to and fro. Tall trees and dense clumps of rushes overhung the sand on either side, and from their dangling branches and stems were suspended the neatly rounded nests of weaver birds. A single cormorant, standing near the water, took off and arrowed away in a hard, flat flight. But the tiny black and white kingfisher, hovering high above the stream, its wings whirring rapidly, ignored the humans completely, continuing its relentless search for fish.

Jess and David crossed the sandbank, their feet scuffing its unblemished surface, and knelt at the stream's edge, leaning their faces to the water and sucking it straight into their mouths, much as the baboons did. The boy said nothing, but when he came to drink, he first scooped the water up in his hands, and drank as he would have from a cup.

Satisfied, they sat down on the cool shaded sand and faced each other.

"Well?" Jess prompted him.

"I'm thinking you are leaving this place now," the boy said. With surprising delicacy, he reached out and touched Jess's wild and matted hair, then brushed his fingertips against the filthy, greasy material of David's shirt. "Is not good, this thing," he added quietly. "Is time for going home."

"Is that why you came?" David asked, "To persuade us to go back?"

He nodded.

"I take dog from village, the dog for hunting. I am looking two days."

"Then you've wasted your time," David said abruptly.

"Maybe not," Jess cut in. "He can carry a message for us." She addressed the boy directly: "You know the Hunter? The man who's searching for us—the one with the cut on his face? Well, tell him we won't leave here till he gives up the search and stops the shooting. Will you do that?"

"I am doing it, but I think he not listen. Everybody— the police, the mothers, the fathers—they are saying, find this children. They are coming to the village many times, with much crying. And this man, this Hunter, he is looking, looking. Now he is telling them, first I kill this baboons."

"He's actually saying that?" David asked incredulously.

"This is bad animals, he say. They are stealing mealies, they are stealing children. First we kill them, and then the children are coming home. For sure."

"And do people believe him?"

"They are believing."

David and Jess exchanged knowing glances. What the boy said only confirmed their growing conviction about the world beyond the escarpment. It was not theirs at all, not any longer, but the abode of the Hunter. They had come to feel more at home here, within the protective cover of the bush. They looked around themselves appreciatively, strangely gratified by the quietude of the scene: the meandering stream, its surface barely ruffled by the light afternoon breeze; the cloud-flecked sky just visible through the overarching trees; the summer swallows skimming across the water in a zigzag dancing pattern. And further downstream, something they had not noticed until then: a large, white-breasted fish eagle, sitting talon-tense upon a jutting branch, its fierce gaze fixed upon the water below.

Jess turned toward the boy. He appeared suddenly distant from her, different, almost like a visitor from another world.

"Can't the people understand that what the Hunter's doing only makes us want to stay here?" she said. "The other day he killed three baboons, shot them down in cold blood. Does anyone seriously think we'll give ourselves up to him after that?"

The boy clicked his tongue sadly, much as his grandfather had done once before.

"Is very bad," he murmured.

"That's what you've got to make them realize," Jess insisted.

"I am trying. But this Hunter, he is big man. Important. The people, they are listening to him."

"Well, we're not listening," David said. "As far as we're concerned, he's the enemy. And so is anyone who backs him up."

"I'm agreeing. Is bad. But still I think you come back now."

"What for?"

The boy took a deep breath, struggling to find the right words in this language that was not his own.

"Three days ago," he began, "the police are bringing men for this Hunter. Many. With the guns. They say, now we find this children. We kill much baboons and take the children." The boy clenched his hand into a fist to underline his meaning. "My grandfather is telling me this thing and I am saying nothing. I am thinking, I find this children. I bring them to village. So the men are making no shooting. The trouble is finished."

Jess listened patiently, but then shook her head.

"We're really grateful," she said, "for the food, and for your coming here, and everything. But we can't go back. Not yet anyway. You can see that, can't you?"

He shrugged helplessly and stood up.

"I go now," he said, "for telling them this things you say."

They climbed back up to the path where the dog was still waiting. Before leaving, the boy made one more attempt to persuade them.

"I think much trouble is coming here," he said, his voice betraying the depth of his feeling. "Soon they are finding you. The same like me, with the dog."

"Let them try," David said defiantly. "They'll have their work cut out for them now that we've been warned."

"Yes," Jess chimed in, "don't worry about us. We'll stay on the move."

The boy gave them a last regretful look and, after a brief and oddly formal handshake, they parted. Watching him trot forlornly off down the trail, Jess was surprised by an unexpected pang of sadness, as though the boy's going were a final separation from the old, once familiar world. David must have experienced much the same feeling, because he said wistfully:

"I wish he could have stayed longer, don't you? Though I don't suppose that's the point, not now."

"No, our job's to get the troop moving. From here on we can't afford to stay in one place for too long. We have to keep the Hunter guessing."

Yet despite the briskness and determination with which she spoke, she staggered slightly as she tried to walk away.

"Are you all right?" David asked.

She shook her head, trying to clear the sudden fuzziness.

"Yes . . . fine . . . I'm fine."

But she continued to sway unsteadily, her face covered with a clammy slick of perspiration. It was almost as if her own body, like the poor farm boy who had just left, were giving her a warning.

She tried to tell herself that the dizziness was nothing, that it would soon pass, but by early evening it was obvious that she had some kind of fever. Her stomach ached, all her joints were sore, and she felt alternately cold and hot.

"A good night's sleep will do the trick," she insisted. "I'll be as good as new tomorrow."

David was less confident, and when they stopped for the night he chose their campsite with care, selecting a well-shaded spot close to water. He was equally careful about the erection of a shelter. Instead of the usual makeshift affair, he cut saplings and lashed them together to make a simple skeleton structure. Over this he put strips of bark and layer upon layer of leafy branches. When he had finished, it was almost completely weatherproof, even without the use of the raincoat. This he spread out inside, having first strewn the hard ground with rushes cut from the nearby stream.

"I don't know what you're making all this fuss about," Jess complained. But she was glad enough to crawl inside once it was completed, and fell immediately into a restless, murmuring slumber.

When he woke her two hours later, she was no better. He had cooked mealies in the hot ashes, but she waved them away.

"I'm too tired and sore to eat," she explained apologetically. "All I want is to rest for a while."

Her speech, he noticed, was slightly slurred.

"Go back to sleep then, Jess," he said gently.

With a filthy piece of rag, which was all that remained of the handkerchief, he wiped the perspiration from her face and afterward returned to the fire.

For the remainder of that night he hardly slept, dozing fitfully and starting awake whenever Jess called out in her sleep. Most of what she said was indistinct, but the word *Hunter* kept cropping up, as did the idea of moving the troop on.

By morning, she was delirious and shivering violently, her whole body bathed in sweat. David, now seriously worried, did the only thing he could. Taking off his shirt, he draped it over her, together with the two light sweaters they had brought with them; then he drew the raincoat around her and buttoned it up. In her delirium she tried to tear the raincoat off, muttering all the while about the Hunter, and David had no option but to hold her down. He was frightened that she would catch a chill in the early morning air; and so, as soon as she was quiet, he braided green rushes to make a soft pliable rope and bound this loosely about her.

For the time being there was no question of her eating anything. But David knew that in her present condition there was a distinct danger of dehydration. She had to drink. That in itself posed a problem, because he had no container in which to carry liquid. Eventually he overcame the difficulty by bringing her water in his mouth, bending over her and allowing it to trickle slowly between his lips.

Occasionally, in his journeys to and from the stream, he heard baboons calling in the near distance. They were never far away because Papio, aware that something was wrong, kept the troop in the vicinity. Twice in the course of the day he visited David and Jess, his old bewildered expression reappearing as he gazed into the darkened shelter at Jess's fevered, restless form. Upi accompanied him on each occasion, yakking anxiously when Jess moaned or called out.

David, feeling very alone and uncertain, was grateful for their company; and that evening he was relieved to see Papio bringing the troop back to their former resting place, not more than a hundred yards from where he and Jess were camped.

For him that second night was more of an ordeal than the first. Jess's condition was actually unchanged; but to David, dog tired after long hours of wakefulness, she seemed worse. The feeling of depression he had been stubbornly keeping at bay gradually forced itself upon him. At some point during the early hours of the morning he finally gave in to it, silently admitting what he had been struggling to ignore: the possibility that Jess might die; that with no one to help them, and he unable to leave her for more than a few minutes at a time, she might slip away from him forever.

"Not her, not Jess," he muttered aloud.

He stood up abruptly and walked away from the fire, gazing up through the trees at the stars scattered randomly across the blackness of the sky. They looked strangely cold, distant, indifferent to everything he and Jess had tried to achieve; and Jess herself seemed to be floating up to meet them, her smooth young skin becoming lost in the eternal blackness that lay beyond. It all felt so unjust, so pointless. Then, as he groped for an answer, for some vestige of meaning behind it all, his mind, fogged by fatigue and worry, lighted on the figure of the Hunter. He saw him as he had appeared on the evening of the first ambush, standing in the narrow neck of the gorge, his rifle trained on the silhouetted shape of Sultan. Except that it was no longer Sultan who was etched against the dying embers of the western sky, but Jess. He, the Hunter, now hovering up there above him, his sinister figure merging into the splayed shape of Orion, seemed intent on snatching Jess away, on drawing her into his own senseless darkness. The Hunter had become truly the minister of death.

To David, tired out and confused, it all suddenly appeared crystal clear, and in that moment of false clarity his attitude to the Hunter changed. His fear of him, his desire to escape, became subtly tinged with malice—the kind of malice that could all too easily deepen into the most destructive hatred.

He hadn't meant to sleep. He had lain down beside the fire intending only to doze for a few minutes. But when he woke it was broad daylight and Jess was calling to him in a feeble, croaky voice. Crawling hurriedly into the shelter, he found that her forehead was cool, her delirium vanished with the night; and unable to prevent himself, he began to cry.

"What is it?" she asked, not understanding at first.

She tried to sit up, but was too weak.

"It's nothing," he said, smearing tears hastily across his cheeks, "it's just that I thought . . . after all day yesterday . . ."

"Yesterday? How long have I been asleep?"

"Two nights and a day."

She understood his reaction then.

"You don't get rid of me that easily," she said, smiling feebly.

But already she was growing tired, slipping back to sleep.

She woke again later in the morning, able to sit up now and eat a little of the baked mealie David brought to her, chewing slowly on the tender pips at the end of the cob. Even that small amount of food seemed to increase her strength and she insisted on going outside, David half-carrying her to the bank of the stream where she lay back on the sand, enjoying the warm sunlight that filtered through the overhanging branches.

With Upi watching over her, fussing around as though

she were another infant to be taken care of, David went off on a hunting trip. He wasn't gone more than a couple of hours, but on his return he found her standing shakily beside the shelter. Her illness had left her thinner than ever, almost emaciated, and with her great shock of unruly hair she looked top-heavy, as though the slightest wind would send her sprawling.

"What are you doing on your feet?" he said impatiently. "You should be resting."

She took several faltering steps and sank down beside the cold ashes of the fire.

"I thought I'd get some practice in," she said. "We'll have to move on tomorrow if we're going to stay clear of the Hunter."

David shook his head.

"Traveling's out of the question for a day or so. You have to get your strength back first. That's why I've been out hunting"—and he held out a collection of dead bush doves. "We need meat to build you up."

Secretly, he suspected that she would be unfit to travel any distance for at least a week. But her resilience surprised him. That evening she ate a hearty meal, and after a good night's sleep she was noticeably stronger.

"You're as bad as Upi," he remarked jokingly. "You never know when you're beaten."

She grinned back at him, her face pinched and thin, her eyes deeply sunken and yet clear and healthy at last.

"Don't worry," she replied, "Upi and I will still be around when you're pushing up the daisies—or the kikuyu grass, or whatever it is they plant over you these days."

Her determination and optimism increased with her growing strength, and that evening she seriously challenged him over the business of moving on.

"It has to be tomorrow," she argued. "It's not fair to the troop, exposing them like this."

"What about being fair to yourself? If you set out too soon, you could have a relapse."

She considered the possibility.

"I'll just have to take the chance," she said doggedly.

"You may want to, but not me. I'm not going through that again, sitting around wondering whether you're about to kick the bucket."

"But the troop . . ."

"I'm thinking about the troop too," he interrupted her. "If you have a relapse, they'll be stuck here even longer."

He saw her hesitate and used it to his advantage.

"One more day, that's all I'm asking. It's not much. Then I promise we'll get out of here, even if I have to carry you."

She didn't answer immediately.

"Well?" he said.

"I guess it would make sense . . ."

"Then it's a bargain? One more day?"

"All right, another day," she said, finally relenting.

The decision made, she tried to put it out of her mind, yet for hours afterward she was haunted by the feeling that she had made a mistake by giving in so easily. How fatal a mistake, she had as yet no idea.

FOURTEEN

Late in the afternoon of her third and final day of convalescence, they again heard the baying of a dog in the distance. It was a well-fed, sturdier animal this time, followed not by a boy, but by a man dressed in khaki, a rifle slung over his shoulder. David caught a glimpse of him and went running back to warn Jess.

"Is it the Hunter?" she asked, starting up at the news.

"No, but he's dressed the same."

"Then we have to lead the troop away from here."

"We can't, it's too late. They'll never move with dusk coming."

"Then they have to hide in the trees."

As the sound of the dog's baying grew louder, they were already doing that, and Jess and David soon joined them, sitting hunched and still in the fork of one of the lower branches. They didn't have long to wait: Within minutes the dog came running into view, followed closely by the man. A chorus of protest rang out from the watching baboons, and the man, after glancing up into the trees, called the dog over and clicked a lead onto his collar.

Jess and David had feared he would start shooting

right away, but he didn't even slip the strap of the rifle from his shoulder. With the dog now firmly under control, he began to survey the area, working his way methodically around the grove of tall trees in which the baboons were hidden. Toward the end of that careful inspection he spotted the shelter that David had built days earlier and went over to examine it. The only thing left there was the raincoat, still spread over the strewn rushes, and the man dragged it out, a look of satisfaction on his face. Folding it up, he tucked it into his belt and came back to the grove of trees.

"He knows we're here now," Jess whispered.

Yet he made no attempt to communicate with them. With the flaming ball of the setting sun just visible through the trees behind him, he sat down near the bank of the stream and lit a cigarette. He continued to smoke quietly as the sun sank from view and the shadows of evening flowed together to form darker and darker pools. Soon he was no more than a dim outline, the tip of his cigarette glowing like a fierce red eye in the gathering twilight. Still watching tensely, Jess and David saw that glowing tip arc away and vanish in the stream.

"Now what?" David murmured.

The man had risen to his feet, but instead of coming nearer, he simply turned his back and walked off toward the north, with the dog beside him.

The dusk was well advanced by now, stars appearing one by one, the soft dark blue of the sky changing slowly to deep black.

"It's a trick," Jess whispered. "He's waiting somewhere just out of sight. He'll be back in a minute."

But apart from the clatter of insects, no other sound disturbed the silence. When the moon, almost at the full, rose high enough to send its light filtering down through the leafy canopy, it revealed no sign of him.

"I don't like it," David said uneasily, "sitting down there all that time and then just walking off."

"What do you think he was up to?"

"Hard to say for certain. He might have been standing guard, just making sure the troop didn't move off elsewhere. He knew that once it was dark they'd stay put until morning. Which would give him plenty of time."

"Time?"

"To get reinforcements. Maybe to bring the Hunter here."

Jess let her breath out between her teeth with a faint hiss.

"We'll have to find a way of moving the troop before morning," she said urgently.

"It can't be done, Jess. He knows that, and so do we."

"We could light fires—fire the bush if we had to."

"The bush is too green. In any case, baboons are as scared of fire as they are of the dark. They'd only climb higher."

"There must be something."

"Not that I can see. All we can do is sit here until morning and pray we can move out before the Hunter arrives." He paused and added quietly: "Either that or give ourselves up."

Jess made no response, and together they descended to ground level, making themselves as comfortable as they could beneath the trees. Before them lay a long and anxious night. A fire was out of the question—as too, Jess thought, was sleep. But in her weakened state she soon dropped off, her head lolling heavily onto David's shoulder. Taking care not to wake her, he spread one of the sweaters on the ground and eased her down onto it, putting his own shirt and the other sweater over her. He knew that in his case sleep would be more difficult to come by, and he tried to compose himself for the hours ahead.

Slowly the moon rose higher in the sky, casting its silvery-white light over the silent forest. He waited patiently until it reached its zenith and started on its downward path. Only then did he venture outside the grove. Flashlight in hand, he padded quietly along the game trail down which the hunter had disappeared, following it for several hundred yards, to a ridge that looked out over the surrounding country, before stopping to listen and watch. He didn't remain there long, soon returning to where Jess lay sleeping peacefully; but periodically throughout the rest of the night he repeated that journey.

Toward morning he began to feel more hopeful. The moon had fallen low in the sky and the new day was not far off. There was, he estimated, time for just one more trip along the trail, and after that they could be away, and free.

It took him only minutes to reach the ridge and at first he was so intent on the eastern horizon, searching for traces of dawn, that he overlooked the obvious signs he had come to watch for. Even when he noticed them, he mistook them momentarily for the hard-backed fireflies that sometimes buzzed through the under-growth. Yet these were too numerous for fireflies: scores of tiny lights, strung out in a long line, snaking slowly up through the bush toward the ridge where he now stood. So many of them that he still couldn't quite credit what he was seeing: more like an army than the group of hunters he had expected and feared.

Already he could hear them, the swish of their legs against the grass and leafy bushes that lined the trail, and turning, he ran madly back toward the grove.

"Jess!" he cried, shaking her. "They're coming!"

She started out of a deep sleep.

"What?"

"They're coming! A whole army of them! I couldn't believe my eyes!"

She struggled to her feet, staggering slightly from lingering weakness, while above her the baboons stirred restlessly, grunting to each other across the gulf of darkness.

"An army?" she said, her mind still drugged with sleep, unable to grasp what he was saying.

"Yes, listen!"

She also heard them then: the many footfalls; the sound of skin and clothing brushing against under-growth. The scores of lights that had guided them through the miles of bush were extinguished now they were so close—only the occasional beam of a flashlight indicated the way. There were a few curt commands in a language Jess and David didn't understand, and the shadowy forms of people fanned out around the grove, surrounding it completely.

"Who are they?" Jess whispered.

She and David crept toward the edge of the grove, and in the pale yellowing rays of the setting moon, they saw them: poor farming people from the villages along the edge of the plateau; men, women, and children, armed not with rifles, but with pots and pans, empty metal buckets and kettles, anything that could be rattled and banged. And within the circle of villagers, a knot of armed men, the tall figure of the Hunter among them.

Nobody moved. The baboons, unnerved by this strange disturbance, were locked in fearful silence. The villagers and hunters, having reached their goal, stood like figures carved from shadow. Once, a stick accidentally clashed against a metal pot and someone snapped out a warning. Silence descended once again, while the moon dipped down behind the trees and the eastern sky gradually lightened.

"What are they waiting for?" David muttered.

"Hush!" Jess whispered.

She too was waiting, more terrified by her own forebodings than by the encircling figures. She watched as the moon slid out of sight, leaving behind only the palest of haloes. In the ensuing twilight, uncertain and hazy, neither wholly night nor day—the time Jess ever after associated with the world of the nightmare—the Hunter called out to them. She would have recognized his voice anywhere, its characteristic harsh quality:

"David! Jessica! Are you in there?"

She tried to clap her hand over David's mouth, but he was already answering:

"Didn't you get our message? We don't . . ."

She managed to muffle the rest, but even those few

words had been enough for the Hunter's purposes.

"Good! They're out of the trees," she heard him say. "Everybody ready!"

A scatter of tiny lights appeared among the armed men—not the hand-held flashlights, but small lamps strapped to their foreheads. There followed an untidy rattle of rifles being loaded, and the men, still bunched together, walked straight toward the grove.

"Stop!" Jess shouted desperately. "We're coming out! We're coming out!"

But her voice was lost in the sudden uproar as the villagers began beating at their pots and pans. It was a deafening noise that blotted out everything: Jess's screams of protest; the screeching and yakking of the baboons as they scrambled through the upper branches; the voice of the Hunter as he signaled for his men to spread out in a straight line.

Unable to make herself heard, Jess started running toward the men. She no longer knew whether or not David was beside her—only that she had to stop the Hunter in time. She reached the nearest of the men as he was about to enter the trees. With the lamp burning on his forehead and his features sunk in shadow, he appeared faceless, a creature without eyes or ears. She had meant to plead with him, to make him call a halt, but when the cold probing eye of the lamp swung toward her, the head behind it featureless and insentient, she was speechless for a moment, too taken aback to resist as a hand snatched at her, grasping her tightly by the wrist—and a voice, hoarse and triumphant, called out something that was lost in the general din.

With the cool touch of those fingers upon her flesh, dragging at her, she found her voice:

"The Hunter!" she yelled. "He has to stop them! Has to . . . !"

Somewhere close by there was a loud explosion, followed by another and another. Only feet from where she stood, a twisting fragment of once living shadow came crashing down through the branches and landed with a thud that seemed to shake the ground beneath her. She tried to reach out toward the still form, tears of pain and dismay pouring down her cheeks, but the man was pulling at her, trying to force her away from the grove. Turning savagely upon him, she sank her teeth into his wrist, clamping hard upon the bone; and as he released her and leapt back, she dived off into the trees.

Guided only by the tiny lamps that bobbed tantalizingly through this twilit world, she groped her way forward, bumping into trunks of trees, falling, scrambling, and blundering on. The explosions were bursting out all around her now, one after the other, and the screeching of the baboons had risen to a point where it could be heard even above the uproar. A second twisted shape came hurtling down, landing almost at her feet. She went sprawling across it, the slack body warm and soft against her own. Horrified, she tried to push it from her, her hands slipping through the warm, wet fur. With a scream, she jerked her hands away and rolled clear, wiping her palms and fingers hurriedly on the ground, her ragged jeans, her bare upper body . . . anywhere that would clean them, rid them of that hot cloying touch.

She stumbled on through the fading darkness, having forgotten whatever it was she had been searching or hoping for, wanting only to break out of this ring of noise and death. More bodies fell from high in the can-

opy, dying hands grabbing, jerking at the delicate fili-
gree of branches that spread themselves against the
lightening sky—the stars winking out one by one as
the nerveless shapes came tumbling down. Yet another
landed directly in her path, twisting where it lay,
groaning. The beam of a headlamp spotlighted it, as
though for her special benefit, and she saw Gray, jaws
agape in agony, lying contorted on the ground before
her. There was a terrible wound in her stomach. Gray
clawed at it with one hand, while with the other she
groped blindly for the infant that crouched just beyond
her reach, too petrified to move, blinking spasmodi-
cally in the blinding light.

Jess hurled herself at the lamp, tripped and fell, her
hands closing on a heavy length of stick. She rose swiftly,
swinging the stick in a wide arc, the two movements
blending into one as the wood came into shuddering
contact with the dim outline that towered above her.
In all that noise there was no cry of pain or protest.
The dim outline wavered and dissolved, the merciful
darkness rushing back as the lamp went spinning off
into space. A second later Jess was groping on the
ground—encountering first the now lifeless body of
Gray; and then touching, tenderly scooping up, the much
smaller body that quivered and squirmed within her firm
grasp.

The feel of that tiny scrap of life, the hands and feet
clinging to her arm, steadied her. She looked about her,
saw the pale light of the eastern sky, and headed in the
opposite direction, deliberately choosing the path of
darkness. The brutal crash of rifle fire continued on every
side, spidery figures toppling from the sky as the lights

bobbed and weaved. But Jess knew where she was going now and nothing deflected her. Twice more, lamps loomed up immediately ahead, and on each occasion she lashed out with the stick, the tall shapes staggering away, leaving her path open. Once, she thought she heard David calling to her, straining above the tumult, yet even that did not make her pause or turn aside.

She slipped between the trees on the outer edge of the grove and confronted the line of villagers. As soon as she appeared they ceased their banging and clattering and stood facing her. There was nothing threatening or formidable about them. They were just poor farming people, barefoot, dressed in worn and ragged clothing, their faces tired and drawn in the faint gray light of morning. Yet to Jess's eyes, now clouded with the darkness of bitter experience, they had become the enemy; each of them guilty of the blood that stained her hands; all of them, whether short or tall, male or female, bearing the hated imprint of the Hunter. Whirling the stick above her head, she forced them aside and ran off into the lingering shadows, as though she were intent on pursuing the night itself.

David found her less than an hour later, in an overgrown gully about two miles from the grove. His own cheeks were smeared with tearstains, though now he was stern faced. Jess was still crying, her breath coming in racking sobs that made her whole body shudder. She was crouching on a stony patch of ground, the lifeless body of Gray's child lying between her feet. He bent down and took the body gently in both hands. In the broad light of day he could see clearly what Jess, in the darkness, had been unaware of: the peppering effect of a gunshot wound down one side.

"They killed it!" she choked out. "They killed it!"

She repeated those three words over and over again, as though the death of that tiny child were the sum total of the night's disaster.

"Listen to me, Jess," he said, trying to reason with her. "We can't stay here. It's too dangerous."

She ignored him, intoning the same words softly to herself, exactly as if she were alone.

With quick deliberate movements he placed the body back on the ground and took her fiercely by the shoulders, shaking her until her head lolled helplessly from side to side. Yet she still refused to acknowledge him.

"Jess?" he pleaded, "Jess?"

When she still didn't answer, he hit her hard across the side of the head, almost knocking her over.

She looked up then, seeing him clearly at last. Behind him was a small group of gray-brown figures, among them, miraculously, the familiar shapes of Papio and Upi. Though now was not the time for elation.

"Come," he said simply, and she rose and followed him and the remnant of the troop along the edge of the gully.

How far they ran, and in what direction, she had no idea. The next thing she knew, the sun was high overhead and she was lying facedown on a soft bed of forest litter. Upi was stretched out beside her, struggling for breath, so exhausted that for the moment she had allowed her child to slip from her grasp. Jess sat up and looked about her. Papio was seated a little higher up the slope, and around him were grouped what was left of the troop. There were less than twenty baboons in all, most of them juveniles, small and agile enough to have slipped through the Hunter's net. Of the larger, more senior animals, only two remained: Ma, as quiet and imperturbable as ever; and Cyclops, gazing warily at the surrounding bush with his one good eye. The rest—Scruffy, Muscles, Dusty, and a host of others—had apparently perished with Gray.

Jess stood up and walked down the slope to where David was perched on a ledge of rock, watching the valley below. He glanced over his shoulder as she approached.

"Is this all?" she asked tonelessly.

He nodded, without looking at her.

"I rounded up as many as I could . . . as many as got through."

"But less than twenty out of a hundred and fifty!"

"It was the best I could do."

They were silent for some time, Jess biting her lip and staring at the ground. When she raised her eyes, she noticed for the first time where they were: not close to the Zambezi, as she had assumed, but high up on the side of the valley.

"Why did you bring us up here?" she asked.

"Because it's the last thing they would have expected. They'll be searching for us down there."

"But they'll realize their mistake eventually, and there's so little cover as high as this."

He turned toward her, his eyes unyielding, his face pale with barely contained hatred.

"Do you want to go on running, Jess? Just running and hiding until this happens all over again?"

She shook her head.

"Then tell me what you do want."

His eyes were fixed on her face, challenging her; but not for a second did she hesitate. It was, after all that had occurred, so easy for her to answer him.

"I want the Hunter," she said simply.

He grinned for the first time that day—a grim, strangely hostile expression, totally bereft of joy.

"Me, too. I don't care what it costs, just as long as he pays. Him and everybody who helped him."

Jess moved instinctively closer to David, their bare shoulders touching in the warm sunlight.

"How can we do it?" she asked. "The Hunter's armed, and we have nothing now."

He gave her the same wolfish grin.

"I've been thinking about that and I've decided it's time we turned the tables on him."

"Can we do it?"

"I think so."

"How?"—that one word bursting from her lips like the explosive, warning bark of a baboon.

"I'll show you."

FIFTEEN

As night was falling they left what remained of the troop in the shelter of the cliffs and climbed up the zigzag path to the plateau above. It was dark when they reached the top, a sprinkle of stars showing overhead, the moon a cold, watchful presence in the cloudless sky, casting its uncertain light on the flower-crested rows of mealies.

"How do we know the Hunter won't be there?" Jess asked as they paused for breath.

"We don't. That's the chance we have to take."

Together, they stepped through the fringe of tall grass and out on to the cleared tract of land at the edge of the field. The tiny village settlement was close at hand: a fire burning within the circle of mud huts, a few shadowy figures around it.

"Looks peaceful enough," David murmured.

He had hardly spoken when the silence was shattered by the sound of furious barking and a group of dogs came lunging out to meet them. This time he and Jess were expecting such a reception, and before the dogs were well clear of the huts they were met by a hail of stones and clods of earth that drove them, yelping, back into the shadows.

David and Jess edged forward, pausing only when they reached the outskirts of the village—waiting patiently in the silvery darkness as a small lamp bobbed out toward them.

They recognized the boy first, his familiar face visible in the light of the hurricane lamp that he was holding aloft. The old man was standing behind him, a blanket draped across his shoulders, the battered rifle clutched in one hand.

"Why are you coming?" the boy asked.

"We're giving ourselves up," Jess said, "we've had enough."

The boy did not smile or seem pleased, as she had expected. He merely looked concerned, no longer trying to hide the shock he felt at their wild, half-naked appearance.

"I am very glad for this," he said simply.

He spoke quietly to his grandfather, and the old man, equally serious, nodded his approval. Motioning for them to follow, he took the lamp and led the way back into the village.

A group of women and small children were standing around the fire. The women clicked their tongues with dismay as Jess and David appeared, and instantly made room for them. One of the babies, not more than two years old, hid his face in his mother's skirt and began to cry—letting out a series of muffled wails that made Jess shudder and draw closer to the comfort of the flames.

"You sit now," the boy said, and brought from one of the huts a pair of low three-legged stools, placing them side by side in the dust.

They murmured their thanks and sat down, smiling vacantly as they had done all along. Yet beneath this guise they were fully alert, taking careful note of everything about them: the large black pot suspended over the fire; the exact position of the dogs now lying peacefully in the shadows; the way the old man tottered over to the nearest hut and leaned the rifle against the rough mud wall.

"I am thinking maybe you are being sick some time," the boy said, addressing Jess.

"No, I'm fine."

"But thin, the body very thin."

"I had a touch of fever, that's all. It's gone now."

"Ah, the fever."

He explained to the listening women who shook their heads understandingly. One of them disappeared for a few moments, returning with a blanket that she placed around Jess's shoulders.

"Warm," she said falteringly, "warm."

Jess didn't bother to thank her, conscious suddenly of David's foot touching hers. She nodded, almost imperceptibly, and David stood up, making an elaborate show of stretching and yawning.

"Too hot for me, a fire like this," he said. "Not what I'm used to. Makes me sleepy."

He moved back a yard or two, in the direction of the nearest hut. As he did so, Jess also stood up and calmly tossed one of the wooden stools into the fire. There were cries of alarm as several figures darted forward to drag it clear, and by the time the noise and excitement had died down, David was standing with the battered .303 rifle cradled in his arms.

"All right," he said, no longer smiling, "where do you keep the rest of the ammunition for this thing?"

The dogs, bristling and growling, had risen from their hollows in the dust; and the old man, muttering angrily, advanced a few paces, stopping only when David shook the rifle in his direction.

"There are other people besides the Hunter who can use one of these," he said threateningly.

Only the boy understood his actual words, but the tone was clear enough. There was a shocked silence that seemed to intensify as Jess came and stood at David's side—the two of them grimly facing the half-circle of villagers.

"Come on," he said coldly, "where's the ammunition?"

Several of the children had begun to whimper. Their mothers quickly gathered them up and comforted them.

"You!"—David pointed straight at the boy. "Show me!"

The boy didn't move, watching him with troubled eyes.

"Why you do this thing?" he asked. "Is no good for you."

"If the Hunter can do it, so can we!" Jess burst out.

"Is no good for you," he repeated stubbornly.

Jess snatched the rifle from David and nodded toward the huts.

"They're not going to help us," she said bitterly, "they're on the Hunter's side. You'd better look for yourself."

Lamp in hand, he went from hut to hut. In the third one he found what he was after: three small yellowing

178

boxes wrapped in a square of oiled cloth. He took them out to Jess, together with two blankets and several boxes of matches.

"This should keep us going for a while," he said.

"What about food?"

"Not a bad idea."

With Jess covering him, he peered into the black pot hanging over the fire. It was half full of nshima, the sticky white mealie porridge that formed the basis of the villagers' diet. In a smaller pot, warming in the ashes, was a heap of cooked talapia, a wide-bodied fresh water fish that abounds in the rivers.

"This'll do," he said, and dragged both pots over to where Jess was standing.

Kneeling side by side in the dust—Jess still with one hand on the gun—they began cramming the food into their mouths, tearing pieces from the fish with their teeth and scooping up the nshima by the fistful. Nobody spoke while they were eating, but the troubled look on the boy's face had grown more pronounced. Without being asked, he picked up an old plastic jug half full of water and carried it over to them. David took a long drink, wiped his chin on the back of his hand, and again crammed his mouth with nshima.

"You not this animals," the boy said with quiet reproval, and pointed out into the darkness, "not this baboons."

Jess spat a mouthful of food back into the pot and stood up.

"You think they're worse than you are?" she said disgustedly.

"Not bad," the boy corrected her gently, "different."

"Yes, so different from you that they don't try and butcher the other creatures they share this country with."

"I not this butcher," the boy said. "I go to you. I say, much trouble, you come now. But you stay, and the Hunter is shooting."

"Oh, so I suppose now the shooting was our fault!" Jess retorted, her voice rising almost to a shout.

Suddenly, unaccountably, she felt close to tears.

"Is not your fault, is not my fault," the boy said calmly.

"That's where you're wrong. It is your fault. It was your people, the farmers around here, who helped the Hunter."

"Is true they are helping," the boy conceded. "They do this many times. When the baboons are taking the mealies, the Hunter comes. He say, we go now for shooting them."

"Yes, but this time they weren't taking your stupid mealies, were they?" David broke in.

The boy shrugged.

"Many baboons now. Too many. The Hunter is shooting them some time. For sure. Is sad, this thing. But . . ."

He shrugged again.

"Sad!" Jess burst out. "He calls it sad!" With her foot, she upended the large pot, emptying the rest of the nshima into the dust. "I suppose you think that's sad too. Except that tomorrow morning you'll cook some more."

The boy stared evenly back at her.

"Tonight the children are hungry," he said reprovingly.

"And tonight—out there—the baboon children are dead!"

Jess turned away, her thin dark body trembling violently. The boy too had turned away, his eyes downcast.

"I am very sorry . . ." he began, but David cut him short.

"That's enough of that!" he said abruptly.

With the butt of the rifle he struck the bottom of the pot several times. It was made of cast iron, and at the third blow it shattered and caved in. One of the women, seeing first the food and now the pot totally ruined, started to scream at him, but he ignored her.

"Take a good look at that," David instructed the boy. "It's nothing but rubbish now. Well, you show it to the Hunter and tell him that's what we think of him."

Jess, much calmer, turned back toward them.

"Don't forget the other message," she said.

"Oh, yes. And tell him that if he tries to follow us, this is what he can expect."

David pointed the barrel upward and pulled the trigger. The subsequent recoil almost tore the rifle from his hands. But the feeling of violence was oddly gratifying, as was the deafening roar that shattered the silence of the night. The dogs pelted off between the huts; and the villagers, struck with terror, threw themselves facedown onto the ground—while David and Jess, unobserved, slipped silently away into the night.

They were safely within the cover of the bush before the sound of the children's crying reached them. Neither felt troubled by it. In any case, it quickly faded as, one behind the other, they slithered down the long zigzag path. At the bottom they turned east, following a game trail for nearly half a mile, and then pausing to rest before beginning the climb up the steep cliff face. In the bright moonlight it was not a difficult climb, and within minutes they heard Papio's welcoming grunt and saw the dark outline of his head peering down at them, the points of the electrodes twinkling feebly.

The whole troop now fitted easily onto a single narrow ledge, and it hurt Jess and David anew to see just how small a number there was. Fortunately they were too tired to dwell on such feelings—Jess especially, who had not yet recovered her full strength. Finding an empty space among the sleeping animals, they wrapped themselves in the stolen blankets and lay down on the bare rock, David still with his hand on the stock of the rifle.

Their arrival had caused hardly any disturbance among the resting troop. Even Papio soon settled back to sleep. Only Upi, with her usual motherly concern, came over to greet them. Crawling carefully along the narrow ledge, she stopped beside Jess and nuzzled her face, licking a trace of nshima from her cheek.

"Good girl," Jess murmured, stroking her muzzle.

Climbing over Jess, she was about to give David a similar greeting when her foot touched the cold, hard barrel of the rifle. She bent down and sniffed at it, licked it with her tongue. The harsh metallic taste made her jerk her head back quickly. She sniffed at David's hand, as though seeking reassurance, but there too she detected the lingering flavor of the metal. With an awkward spring, she leapt back over Jess, brushing her body as she passed, and returned to her place at the far end of the ledge.

Jess, momentarily disturbed, rolled over. Thinking Upi was still beside her, she muttered sleepily:

"You know something, Upi? You're worth more than all those people out there put together."

At the sound of her own name, Upi glanced across at the sleeping humans. But she didn't attempt to approach them again, the alien taste of the metal still fresh upon her tongue. Instead, she put both arms around her adopted young one, drawing it tightly against her—her small round eyes, strangely haunted and lost, staring out across the moon-drenched valley.

SIXTEEN

David slid down the steep track to where they were waiting.

"Quiet as could be up there," he said. "Just a herd of goats in the grass along the edge."

"Goats?" Jess inquired. "Wasn't anyone with them?"

"Not that I could see. Anyway, we have the gun." He brandished it proudly.

Upi, squatting against the rocky hillside, yakked softly, but nobody noticed her reaction.

In single file they slowly ascended the track. There was only a strip of grass at the top, interspersed with the occasional umbrella-shaped thorn tree. The neat rows of mealies began just beyond this strip, the ragged crests nodding lazily in the light breeze, the broad green leaves aglow with morning sunlight. Just visible above the tallest plants, and several hundred yards distant, were the thatched roofs of a small settlement. But the landscape was deserted except for the goats David had referred to. They lifted their heads to gaze at these unlikely intruders; then, unconcerned, went back to nibbling at the grass.

"How's it look?" David asked.

"Fine, except for the goats. Isn't it weird that no one is with them?"

"Don't ask me. I'm no expert."

Jess bit her lip thoughtfully. Something about the situation made her uneasy. Also, the baboons were edgy, though that could easily have been a natural response to the open landscape.

"All right," she said at last, "I guess it's as good a place to start as any."

Crouching low, they led the troop across the grassy strip and into the mealie field. Surrounded by so much food, the baboons soon forgot their nervousness and, with satisfied grunts, settled down to the business of gorging themselves. Jess and David, meanwhile, collected enough mealie cobs for their immediate needs. That took only a few minutes, and with time on their hands they began working along the rows snapping the stems of every third or fourth plant. Before long they had ruined a quarter of an acre or more.

"That probably won't stop them from harvesting the crop," Jess said, wiping sweat from her forehead, "but it'll give them a taste of what they can expect from now on."

"Yes," David agreed, "a kind of warning."

They were still surveying their handiwork when they were startled by a sound behind them—but it was only the goats that had wandered into the field and were feeding on the bright green leaves. Even David scratched his head in puzzlement now.

"I'm sure this isn't supposed to be happening," he said.

"They probably let them into the fields after the harvest," she replied, "but not at this stage."

"So what's going on?"

To his surprise, Jess suddenly began to laugh—a high-pitched, not altogether happy sound.

"Who cares?" she said. "At this rate we won't need to raid their fields. The goats will do it for us."

"You mean an animal rebellion?" he said, joining in the laughter. "With the Hunter as Little Boy Blue, too sleepy to chase the goats out of the corn."

At the mention of the Hunter, Jess grew serious.

"Maybe we'd better think about making a move," she suggested. "Someone's going to come wandering by before long."

Without either of them knowing it, however, one of the village women had already seen the goats entering the field. Shaking her head with vexation, she came hurrying over, intending to chase them out—only to be met by the sight of the feeding baboons.

The first Jess or David knew of her presence was when they heard her shriek and, seconds later, saw her go rushing past only a few rows from where they stood.

"Come on," Jess whispered, "time to move."

But David held her back.

"Hold on. Perhaps this is the sort of situation we should take advantage of."

He was wearing the same thin, wolfish expression as when he had first suggested the attack on the village, and she understood immediately what he was getting at.

Creeping silently from the field, they took up a position in the grass, lying flat on their stomachs so they couldn't be seen. A group of villagers soon came running along the strip of uncultivated land at the edge of the field. As David had suspected, they had no guns: only stone-filled gourds, which they rattled vigorously as they ran.

The baboons, roused from their feeding, began to show signs of agitation. But Jess and David barely spared them a glance, all their attention on the oncoming villagers.

"Wait," Jess murmured, "wait . . . now!"

David jumped up when they were no more than thirty yards away, leaping out directly in their path and firing over their heads.

The effect on the villagers was exactly as if they had run into an invisible barrier. They stopped dead in their tracks, two of the women pitching forward onto their hands and knees, one of the men throwing himself sideways and scrabbling frantically in the soft earth as though trying to dig a hole in which to hide. Then they were all on their feet again, slipping and colliding with each other as they ran for their lives.

Jess let out a loud, oddly forced laugh. The spectacle of the terrified villagers, contrary to her expectations, gave her no pleasure. It left her with only a sour, unpleasant aftertaste. David, also, showed no sign of enjoyment.

"That'll teach them!" he yelled unconvincingly.

With an almost morbid determination, he reloaded the rifle, intending to fire again—as though with that second shot he hoped to dispel the feeling of hollowness inside him. Before he could pull the trigger there was a savage roar from close by.

In their desire for revenge, they had both forgotten

the troop. They turned around and there, at the edge of the field, was Papio, the other baboons clustered fearfully about him.

"It's all right, boy," David said soothingly.

For the first time ever, his words had no effect. Raising his head, Papio roared again, his lips drawing back in a menacing snarl as he reared up on his hind legs.

"It's the gun!" Jess hissed out.

David cast it aside and held out his empty hands, murmuring endearments as he moved slowly forward. But still Papio was not to be placated. Swinging his head from side to side, he edged suspiciously away, grunting menacingly all the while.

"Here," Jess said, "let me have a try."

This time, Papio didn't draw back, allowing her to crouch beside him.

"There . . . there . . ." she whispered, stroking his head.

Gradually he quieted down, his body, which had shivered at the first touch, growing calm and still. Not until he was completely recovered did she stand up and walk toward the lip of the escarpment. He followed her, though he continued to watch David suspiciously, skittering aside the moment David retrieved the gun.

"He got a little scared, that's all," Jess said, as she led them down the steep path.

David nodded. "I'd forgotten how close he was," he admitted. "Still, this is only the beginning. He'll get used to the noise in time."

As their words implied, Papio's response to the rifle shot was for them a matter of minor importance— something that passed out of their thoughts before they reached the bottom of the path. Yet to the small herd boy, who had deserted his goats and had been hiding in one of the thorn trees ever since David's first appearance, it made a marked impression. So much so, that later that day, after the Hunter had been summoned to the village, he faithfully recounted to him the whole incident. The Hunter listened attentively. The result was that, when he set out alone to follow David and Jess's tracks early the next morning, he was equipped not only with his rifle but also with the certain knowledge of what now had to be done.

At first they didn't realize it was the Hunter. They were resting in the open, and suddenly there he was: a distant, khaki-clad figure, calling to them.

Without a word they slipped back into the brush, traveling in an easterly direction, following the hard veins of rock that had been exposed by erosion on the upper parts of the slope. In spite of their care, an hour later he appeared again, much closer this time, calling to them as before.

"Who is it?" Jess asked, thinking it might be the man who had tracked them with the dog.

"We'll soon find out," David said.

While the others continued up a steep rocky gully he climbed the nearby ridge and waited. Within minutes the man came into view, moving more quickly than the troop, but having to stop frequently to check the ground at his feet. He was a powerfully built figure, carrying a light backpack, and with a pair of binoculars slung around his neck. His face could not easily be seen because he had on a broad-brimmed khaki hat. When he was almost immediately below David, he raised his head and looked about him, as though sensing that he was being watched—and on his left cheek was the angry red mark of a recent wound.

David ducked out of sight and ran hard until he caught up with the others.

"It's the Hunter," he said breathlessly.

Jess gave him a doubtful look.

"Are you sure? This isn't the way he works."

"I tell you it's him."

"What's he up to then? Why did he stand out in the open like that, calling to us?"

These were questions they could not answer for the moment. All they could do was press on as fast as Upi's faltering heart would allow. Yet no matter how quickly they went, nor how much they back- or side-tracked, he drew steadily closer, shouting to them whenever he had the opportunity.

All that afternoon he followed them—calling across hillsides, down gullies, from the tops of ridges. Only in the deepening dusk did they manage to shake him off and camp in peace. Soon after dawn, however, he again picked up their tracks and the whole business began once more. Except that this time, Upi, already tired from the previous day's journey, was soon in a distressed state. By midday she was beginning to fall so far behind that David and Jess were forced to carry her from time to time. Now they were not so much running away as slogging doggedly on, with the Hunter's voice always there in the background.

"I can't figure it out," Jess said during one of their rests. "He could easily get ahead of us and cut us off. Why doesn't he?"

"He's up to something," David replied angrily, "and whatever it is, I'm not taking much more. He's going to learn that things aren't the way they used to be."

He tried to carry out that threat an hour later, little realizing at the time that he was playing into the Hunter's hands—that he was merely enacting his part in a drama that the Hunter had conceived of in the few minutes he had spent listening to the herd boy.

It was the hottest part of the day, the sun beating down from a milky-blue sky. The spot they had chosen was, from their point of view, a good one: a thick clump of bush that could only be approached across a steep open hillside that offered little cover. From the shelter of the deep shade they watched the hated khaki-clad figure emerge from the trees and begin toiling up toward them. They allowed him to cover about half the distance, to reach a point where he was standing on bare rock, with only a few stunted aloes around him; and then David fired directly above his head.

But he was not like one of the villagers, quick to take fright at the sound of gunfire. It was something he was all too familiar with, and swinging his own rifle up, he returned David's shot, the bullet tearing through the trees immediately above where the fugitives lay.

"Damn you!" David muttered, ramming another shell into the breech.

With feverish determination he fired off round after round, the other rifle always answering him like an echo. Gritting his teeth, he clung desperately to the old .303, which bucked and jolted viciously each time he pulled the trigger, lowering his sights a fraction after every shot in an attempt to force the Hunter back. So intent was he on this duel of nerves that he was only dimly aware of Jess shouting at him, striving to make herself heard above the deafening noise. Not until he had exhausted the magazine, and the firing pin clicked on an empty chamber, did he fully register what she was trying to tell him.

"They've gone!" she was yelling, "they've gone!"

He turned around, and where the baboons had been sitting there was only a flattened area of grass. Jess was already running through the bush. He hurried after her and burst out onto a more open part of the hillside. The troop was some way ahead, fleeing from him and Jess as though they themselves had become a mirror image of the Hunter.

"Papio!" Jess screamed out, "Papio!"

At the sound of her voice, he and Upi faltered and stopped, the rest of the troop slowing down and waiting farther up the slope.

"Quick," Jess said, thrusting the blankets at him, "wrap the rifle up in these."

He did as she asked, and they slowly approached the two crouching baboons. Upi yakked at them as they drew near, her canines exposed defensively, growing quiet only when Jess caressed her. Papio was not so easily placated. Even with the gun hidden, he continued to glare at them with fear and distrust. And although he tolerated Jess, the moment David tried to handle him he roared out a protest and backed away. Several minutes of patient, soothing speech were needed before he responded to David's voice; and when he came to him at last, he did so without any sign of the old loving devotion. Rather, he cowered before him as he might have done before a more dominant male baboon—in an act of fearful submission.

The Hunter, meanwhile, watching from below through his powerful binoculars, smiled quietly to himself with satisfaction.

"What we need is rain," David said. "That'd shake him off."

"If you ask me, the rains are over. We haven't seen a dark cloud for ages."

"Anything, then," he said desperately, "as long as it stops him from tailing us. Always there, like a shadow or something."

He looked anxious and distraught, his face showing clearly the strain of the past few days.

"It can't go on like this much longer," she said in an effort to comfort him. "Something's sure to happen soon."

As indeed it did, for not long afterward, halfway up a steep incline, David suddenly staggered and almost fell.

"What's the matter?" Jess asked, as he crouched with his head between his knees.

But she knew the signs all too well, and when she touched his forehead it felt sticky and hot.

"You've got the same fever I had," she told him. "You'll have to rest."

"No," he muttered, "it's better if we keep going."

"But we can't."

He turned on her frantically, his eyes red-rimmed and slightly unfocused.

"If we let the Hunter pin us down, he'll send for

reinforcements. Then you know what'll happen." He pointed meaningfully toward the depths of the valley. "It'll be like that night down there all over again."

She had no answer to that, and in silence she waited for him to recover sufficiently to carry on. He was soon on his feet again, leading the way across a seemingly endless succession of ridges and gullies in their journey eastward. From time to time he would stagger slightly, but he refused to stop. As the fever grew worse, he actually increased his pace, as though trying to keep the sickness at bay by willfully pushing his body to the limit.

"Slow down, David, please," she begged, thinking not only of him but also of Upi, who was showing signs of severe distress.

He shook his head, blundering on, his face streaming with sweat. Upi, sensing the urgency, increased her own effort, her scarred breast heaving in frantic spasms as she strove to keep up.

She also began to stagger as the day wore on, sometimes collapsing altogether, so that Jess had to take her on her back for short periods. On one of these occasions, as Jess bent to lift her, she noticed bloody specks of foam about her lips.

"David!" she called, "I think she's bleeding inside!"

He turned and brushed distractedly at his flushed face.

"Can't stop," he mumbled, "she'll be all right . . . got to lose him . . . the Hunter . . ."

He lurched away, almost falling in his haste, everything but the need to outdistance their pursuer banished from his mind. And Jess, with Upi draped across her shoulders, stumbled after him.

Jess was never more glad to see the sun sink below the horizon than she was that day. David by now was hardly aware of his surroundings, and Upi had begun to cough up clots of blood. Jess herself was near the limits of her strength; but as the Hunter called out yet again, his voice carrying mockingly through the early dusk, she determined to make one last effort, pinning all her faith on the approaching night.

Immediately below them was a dried-up watercourse, lined for some distance on either bank by a tangle of lush growth. As the twilight deepened, like fine dust falling from the darkening sky, she took David's hand and led him down into what she realized might well be their last sanctuary. Even having gained the shelter of this dense bush, she still didn't stop, threading a path along the watercourse until the shadows were so thick about them that the baboons were yakking softly, their frightened eyes gleaming in the last remnants of light.

She called a halt beside a shallow muddy pool. Having all drunk their fill of the lukewarm, faintly gritty water, they took refuge under a narrow slab of rock that, during the height of the rainy season, probably formed the upper level of a small waterfall.

David, his head lolling drunkenly, flopped down on the sand and was soon asleep. The rifle was still clutched in his hand, and Jess pried it loose before covering him with blankets. Upi she placed carefully beside him, thankful for the darkness that prevented her seeing the dried blood that caked the fur of her muzzle. Upi's baby had hours earlier been taken over by Ma, who sat close by, nursing it lovingly. In the faint starlight, Jess could see its small, nearly naked face peering out upon a world that had exposed it to a relentless succession of hardship and disaster.

Too tired to eat the mealies they had brought in the rolled-up blankets, Jess lay back and stared up past the narrow overhang of rock at the night sky. Although she didn't realize it, she saw the broad arch of the heavens much as David had perceived it more than a week before: not as a vast warm cave, the stars, like loving eyes, watching silently as the world slept; but as a distant, indifferent expanse of utter blackness, hopeless, the stars like glittering chips of ice. She closed her eyes, blotting them out—and immediately felt a warm presence beside her.

It was Papio, the electrodes on his head gleaming faintly, mirroring the starlight and making nonsense of her recent vision. Ignored by her throughout the day and, to her deep regret, now too fearful of David to approach him unbidden, he had crept close to her just when she needed him most.

"Hello, my lovely," she whispered softly.

Sitting up, she pressed her face to his, brushing her cheek against his warm muzzle. He gave a low, satisfied grunt and licked at her gently, the soft tip of his tongue caressing her forehead, her eyes, her dry cracked lips; his hands reaching up to her unruly mass of hair, fingering it tentatively in what was for him the deepest possible show of affection. Had either of them known it, that all too brief moment was a last, loving farewell. Fortunately they were aware only of each other's nearness, of the comfort that flows from the simple act of touching, while the darkness and the silence enclosed them tenderly.

It was the Hunter, inevitably, who shattered the peace and calm of their brief communion. He had lost them in the failing twilight, but he was sure they could not have gone far. Even more important, he knew from his observations throughout the day that both David and Upi were ill. It was the kind of opportunity he had been waiting for, and crouched in the darkness less than a hundred yards from where his quarry lay, he fired the first of his flares.

There was a loud report, and a ball of reddish light shot high into the air, hovering for a second and slowly drifting down, casting its lurid brilliance upon the surrounding bush.

Jess, startled by the unexpectedness of it, leapt to her feet and watched as the ball of fire floated down toward her, landing with a loud hiss in the muddy pool only yards from where she stood. She knew what the flare was for. It was a signal to the other khaki-clad figures who in all likelihood were waiting at the edge of the plateau somewhere high above. Yet for her it represented so much more than that. With David moaning in his sleep and the baboons cowering back in terror, the flare was a blood-red symbol of the Hunter himself. Too callous and unfeeling to bide his time until dawn, he was arrogantly transforming night into day, striking at them even through the shroud of darkness.

"You! Hunter!" she screamed. "I'm never coming back with you, no matter what you do! D'you hear me?"

There was a low sound of distant laughter, and in a blind rage she rushed over to where David lay and retrieved the rifle. Ramming a shell into the firing chamber, she stood ready, waiting, her whole body trembling with violent expectation. When the second flare rose triumphantly into the sky, she calculated the point from which it had risen and fired directly at where she imagined the Hunter was standing. The recoil jerked her completely off her feet, but she was up in an instant, staggering as she emptied the rest of the magazine into the surrounding night.

As the last echoes died away and silence descended once more, she limped back into the cover of the rock and toppled forward onto her knees. At her approach, the baboons sidled hastily away—Papio, who only minutes earlier had been nuzzling her lovingly, now grunting out his dislike and distrust, Jess's image, in his eyes, suddenly associated with the hated image of the gun.

Jess was too exhausted to notice. In total darkness she sank down beside David, the rifle still cradled almost lovingly in her arms, the hard metal of the bolt pressed against the soft curve of her cheek. Just before she fell asleep, she muttered aloud: "Don't worry, I'll save you. I promise."

It was not clear whether she was talking to David or to Papio. Nor was it clear any longer, even to herself, what exactly it was she meant to save them from.

SEVENTEEN

David was no better in the morning, but neither was
he any worse. Although he was still running a fever, it
had obviously not affected him as badly as it had Jess.
As soon as the first gray light began to encroach upon
the darkness, he pushed aside the blankets and rose unsteadily to his feet.

"Do you think you can keep going?" Jess asked.

He nodded as he knelt beside the pool and splashed
water over his face and hair.

"I'll keep going as long as Upi does," he replied.

Upi had also risen, still breathing hoarsely, but greatly
improved from the previous evening. In complete silence the whole group moved stealthily up the watercourse.

They followed it for almost a mile, taking full advantage of the cover, pausing only when the incline became too steep for either Upi or David. There had as
yet been no sign of the Hunter, which raised their hopes
slightly—though already Upi was beginning to cough
up blood once again. Jess bent down to lift her, but she
moved away, not wishing to be touched while she had
the strength to walk.

"I expect she wants to stay close to Ma and the baby," Jess said, pretending that nothing untoward had happened. Yet inwardly she was deeply hurt, and when she again turned toward the east she did so with a heavy heart.

At that stage she visualized a long, hard day ahead, little realizing how close to the end of their journey they really were. For when they reached the top of the first ridge, they found themselves staring out, not over the endless vista of bush they had grown used to, but a largely barren landscape—the substratum of limestone, never far from the surface on these upper slopes, was now so exposed that the thin topsoil could support nothing more than sparse, tattered thornbush. Apart from the thick forest deep in the Zambezi valley, the only remaining cover was in a shallow basin immediately below them. It could not have been more than several hundred yards across and it ended abruptly in a rocky ravinelike gully.

"I guess the smart thing would be to head south," Jess said doubtfully.

David didn't answer and she understood why, for like him she had a horror of that whole region.

"Then we'll have to go back," she murmured.

But when they turned around, there, on the opposite ridge, was the Hunter. Now he was not alone. Two khaki-clad figures were standing on either side of him— with a number of similar figures spread out along the length of the slope. Most of them were advancing rapidly, like troops going into battle, sweeping forward in a half-circle formation in an attempt to enclose David and Jess. There was no longer any possibility of retreat, and with only one option remaining, Jess led the small band down the side of the ridge and across the narrow dish of bushland toward the ravine.

At the edge of this ravine stood a huge baobab, its thick tentaclelike roots clinging to the stony ground. It was here, under its craggy, angular branches, shielded by its vast trunk, that Jess, David, and the baboons sought their final refuge.

"I feel as though we've come full circle," Jess said—because in size and shape the baobab was astonishingly like the one they had encountered in the mist at the very start of their journey.

"What?" David muttered, not understanding. His eyes, burning with fever, were wavering from side to side as he struggled to focus clearly.

Jess laid her hand flat on the smooth gray trunk and tried to smile at him.

"It's as if we'd been out for an early morning walk," she said wryly, "and come back to the same place we started from."

She gave a short bitter laugh, for she knew that in truth both she and David were totally different from the two who had first groped their way through the mist and clambered over the roots of the baobab. It was not just a case of their now being filthy and bedraggled or suffering from fever. The real difference went far deeper than that. Like the tortuous roots of the baobab itself, Jess felt twisted up inside, unsure of who and where she was, and strangely daunted by the challenge that lay before her.

"Don't mind me, I'm talking nonsense," she said to David who was still gazing at her in bewilderment.

Brushing the lank, greasy hair from his eyes, she put both arms about him and eased him down into a sitting position. There was little she could do for Upi, who lay on her side, gasping painfully, her lungs rupturing from the constant strain, so that her muzzle and breast were streaked with fresh blood in a way that was distressingly reminiscent of the death of Sultan.

"My poor darling," Jess murmured, forcing back the tears that welled up into her eyes.

She wiped some of the blood away with her fingers, but it did no good—Upi coughed feebly and more trickled from her slack jaws. Suddenly bone weary, Jess leaned back and closed her eyes, trying to ignore everything except the sensation of warm sunlight on her upturned face. There was a brief period of unnatural calm, and then a familiar, hated voice blared out:

"Jessica! David! I'm giving you two minutes before we move in. Make it easy on yourselves. Give up while you have the chance."

Jess jumped to her feet and peered around the tree. The Hunter was standing on a small knoll, megaphone in hand. His companions were grouped around the rim of the basin, ready to close in.

"Why don't you leave us alone?" she shouted. "Just go away and leave us in peace!"

She was distracted by a rustling behind her and she glanced back, expecting to see Papio. But it was David, the rifle gripped tightly in both hands, a wild gleam in his eye as he came lurching toward her.

"That's no use now," she warned him.

She spread her arms wide, to keep him back, but he pushed her aside with surprising force and fired twice, randomly, into the bush, the rifle slamming against his shoulder, twisting him sideways.

"Hunter!" he croaked out threateningly, "I'll show you what'll happen if . . ."

Before he could complete his threat, there was a grating roar from Papio. David and Jess spun around and saw the big male baboon staring at them belligerently. He was no longer the animal they had known but a totally wild creature. Unnerved by the rifle fire, he was backing away, moving instinctively toward the south, to the freedom and shelter of the thick forest.

"No, Papio!" Jess pleaded, "No!"

She rushed forward, pushing her way through the rest of the troop, and tried to fling her arms around his neck, but he lunged at her, the action so minutely calculated that his teeth clicked shut only a fraction of an inch from her arm. Then, while she was still too surprised to cry out, he shoved at her with his powerful shoulder and sent her sprawling. The other baboons streamed past her, eager to desert these strange figures who had shared their lives—leaving behind them only Upi, who had half risen, her bloodstained muzzle drooping wearily between her arms.

"David, you have to stop them!" Jess called desperately.

With a frantic, staggering run, he skirted the baobab and dashed round to the edge of the ravine, cutting off the troop's line of retreat.

"Get back!" he commanded.

The baboons hesitated and stopped—all except for Papio who continued to advance, roaring out a challenge.

"Blast you, Papio!" David yelled dementedly, "I said get back!"

He raised the rifle to his shoulder and pointed it straight at the gaping jaws; while Papio, undaunted, roared again and again. Neither showed signs of giving ground. These two, once such devoted friends, facing each other in the manner of mortal enemies: one, with his finger tightening steadily upon the trigger; the other, his mantle raised, his long canines exposed, threatening to charge at any moment.

Had they been left to themselves, there could have been only one outcome. But before either could commit himself to that last fateful move, there was another, more feeble roar, and Upi came charging toward them. Whether she was intent upon defending David or upon attacking him was never clear. For the last few strides her heart failed, a clot of living red spurting from her mouth as she tumbled in a lifeless heap at David's feet.

Jess would never forget the look of horror on David's face, largely because it mirrored perfectly her own inner turmoil. With a tortured cry he hurled the rifle aside, as though it were hot and burning. She heard it go clattering into the ravine as David, tears and sweat streaming down his face, threw himself onto Upi's body, sobbing as though his heart too were about to break.

It was at that moment that the megaphone again blared out:

"It's all over. Close in."

But it wasn't all over as far as Jess was concerned. Crying and cursing together, she ran to the ravine and slithered down its steep, boulder-strewn side. Somewhere in the background she heard the Hunter call out:

"Two men cut her off. I don't want her getting away again."

It seemed to her at that moment such a strange thing for him to think—that with Upi dead she should still wish to escape. When what she was really after was lying there before her, wedged between two stones, its old wooden stock split right through. Not that the damage mattered—the rifle, like Upi, was at the end of its useful life . . . or nearly so. Just one essential task to be completed. Grasping it firmly, Jess clambered back up out of the ravine.

Papio and the troop had vanished by the time she reached the top. Only David remained, still sprawling across Upi's lifeless body; and hurrying toward them, the Hunter himself.

He could not have been more than twenty yards away when Jess reappeared at the edge of the ravine, the shattered stock of the rifle already clamped against her bare shoulder, the barrel pointing straight at his heart. He slithered to a halt, at first more surprised than scared.

"What the hell are you up to?" he burst out.

She dashed the tears from her eyes.

"Look at what you've done!" she screamed. "Take a last look!"

He realized then what she intended, and a spasm of fear passed across his face, the scar on his cheek crinkling up as his lips drew back from his teeth in a purely animal grimace. It was exactly the way Jess had long dreamed of seeing him—trapped, at bay, his terror written in his eyes. "I want the Hunter," she had once told David. And here he was, helpless before her. Yet now that she had him at her mercy, she felt nothing but emptiness: no elation, no relief, not even a sense of power—his life worthless to her, his lifeblood powerless to bring Upi back from the dead. And although she strained as hard as she could, her whole body trembling with the effort, she found she could not pull the trigger—not even had her own life depended on it.

"Look!" she screamed again, her voice growing more shrill with desperation. "See what you've done! You've killed her!"

Her eyes were swimming with tears, his firm outline running and dissolving in her grief as if he were a painted figure within a make-believe landscape. She could no longer see either him or anything else clearly.

". . . killed her!" she repeated brokenly.

Then David's voice, close beside her, unexpectedly calm and controlled:

"No, Jess. We're the ones who killed her."

It was stated so simply, so directly, that it caught her off guard, and she could not grasp it for a moment.

"What?"

"It wasn't just him. It was us as well. You and me, Jess. We did it together."

Suddenly she knew that it was true—that the circle of their flight, from tree to tree, had been nothing less than the well-trodden path of the Hunter; and that the blood now staining her hands would never wholly be washed away.

She lowered the rifle and let it fall with a clatter at her feet. An instant later, from not far off, she heard Papio's explosive bark, sounding in her ears like a cry of accusation.

"Yes . . ." she broke out miserably, "yes . . ."

EPILOGUE

David's father drove them to the pick up point. He kept glancing across at them, at David especially, his thin face slightly pinched with worry.

"You're sure this is really what you want?" he asked for about the fourth time.

David looked at his father and smiled.

"You mean, can we handle it all right?"

"Yes, I suppose that is what I mean."

David shifted sideways on the seat.

"Listen, Dad, it's not going to be like last time. I promise. It's just that we'll all be leaving here soon, going back to our own countries, and Jess and I will probably never get a chance like this again."

"Oh, I see that . . ." he said hesitantly, ". . . and I do trust you. All that other unfortunate business is behind you now, I know."

They said little more until they reached the headquarters of the Department of Wild Life. There, to the dismay of both Jess and David, they were met by the Hunter. But they soon recovered from their initial shock, because he was nothing like their memory of him. After nearly a year, only the scar remained to identify him, and even that had faded to a thin white line running just below the level of the cheekbone. For the rest, he no longer seemed either very large or very formidable. There was certainly nothing monstrous about his appearance. He actually looked rather ordinary, someone they would have passed in the street without a second glance.

He was waiting for them on the bare earth drive outside the main building.

"We meet again," he said awkwardly and held out his hand.

Although Jess and David felt overcome by embarrassment, they could not bring themselves to shake hands with him.

"No, I suppose you're right," he conceded.

There was a brief, uncomfortable silence and Jess blurted out: "Are you the one who's taking us?"

She had meant her voice to sound neutral, merely curious, but the old hostility was still there.

"I don't think that would be wise, do you?" he said openly, making no attempt to hide what lay between them. "No, it's all been arranged, you'll be going with someone else." He indicated a much taller, thinner man who was walking toward them along the drive. "This is Simon. He's the ranger in charge of that area now, so he'll be leading this particular expedition."

In those first few moments of introduction, Jess and David noticed the same thing about Simon: his sad, oddly perceptive eyes, which lit up as soon as he spoke.

"Well," he said briskly, "shall we make a start?"

He put their two packs in the back of the waiting Land Rover, and after a hurried farewell they were on their way.

Neither of them had been along that road in the intervening period and they felt strange seeing it again, free now of mist and darkness.

"It's a bit like the Hunter," Jess remarked, "not quite the way I imagined it."

"Nothing ever is," David murmured.

"Meaning?"

"Oh, I don't know. Things are always . . . themselves somehow, not how we'd like to make them. I'll be going home soon, back to Australia—I expect that will look different too."

Jess paused before asking the question uppermost in her mind.

"Will you be seeing your mother and brother?"

"Yes."

"And will your parents be . . . ?"

"Getting together again? No, there's no chance of that."

"I'm sorry," she said, conscious of her own tightly knit family and of the settled life in America to which they would all soon be returning.

"So am I," he admitted, "but not the way I used to be. That's one thing I learned from living out here"— and he pointed to the surrounding hillsides. "Everything has a right to be itself. Not just my Mum and Dad. Trees, animals, people, everything. We all have . . . how can I put it? . . . we have to learn to pay for each other's freedom."

Jess considered the idea for a moment or two.

"Yes," she replied pensively, "I think I see it that way too."

They had little opportunity for further conversation, because soon afterward they turned off the main road and went bumping along a rough track. For several miles they wound their way through thick bush; then the landscape leveled out, the bush gave way to open farmland, and a few minutes later they stopped beside a mealie field. Jess and David recognized the place instantly: the small cluster of thatched huts; the cleared section of land at the edge of the field; the vast Zambezi valley visible through the narrow strip of bush.

As they climbed stiffly from the Land Rover, a boy of about their own age walked slowly toward them from the village. He looked taller, thinner perhaps, but otherwise not greatly changed.

They shook hands almost solemnly, mumbling a mixture of greetings and apologies that reminded Jess uncomfortably of their meeting with the Hunter.

"And your grandfather?" David asked. "How is he?"

"He is dead," the boy answered sadly. "He die soon after you are coming here."

"It wasn't because of what we . . .?" David began.

The boy shook his head. "He very old, my grandfather. He say, I am dying when the rain is finished, when all is dry."

"I see."

There seemed nothing more they could say, their chance of apologizing to the old man gone forever. For the second time that day there was an awkward silence. It was Simon who came to the rescue.

"Hurry up," he called, "we have a long walk ahead of us."

They shouldered their packs and for the last time crossed the strip of bush that separated the settled farmland from the wild escarpment country.

Descending the zigzag path was like stepping back in time, reentering another life that still felt so vivid and real that they found themselves looking involuntarily over their shoulders as though half expecting to find Upi or Papio trailing along not far behind. All the old memories came flooding back—the damp, musty smell of the bush after rain; the flocks of tiny white-eyes flitting through the foliage; the egrets, like white shadows, standing poised and still on the open ground or flying gracefully overhead; and always there, in the background, the scream of cicadas.

"Good to be back?" Simon asked.

"Yes and no," Jess replied uneasily. "What about you, David?"

He didn't answer. He was looking intently at the rifle slung over Simon's shoulder, as if he had noticed it for the first time. Jess, following the direction of his gaze, experienced the same sick lurch that she knew he must also have felt.

"Did we have to bring that thing?" he asked.

"What?"

"The rifle."

Simon patted the wooden stock reassuringly.

"It's only a safety measure," he said.

"That's what we thought," Jess said, a trace of the old bitterness creeping back into her voice.

"This is hardly a similar situation," Simon reminded her.

"Yeah, that's true."

But the past, having once been evoked, could not easily be dismissed or forgotten. Like a restless ghost, it seemed to stalk them down the long familiar gullies and across the crests of ridges, almost as tangibly there as the speckled shade that stirred in the light afternoon breeze. So that for the remainder of the day they plodded on in gloomy silence.

They reached their destination as dusk was falling. Neither Jess nor David had asked Simon much about the place itself, and they were taken aback to find it was the pool beside which Sultan had been fatally wounded.

"We can't stop here!" Jess said angrily.

"Why's that?"

"We can't that's all."

"No, not here," David added.

Simon looked carefully at them both, then took out a short-stemmed corncob pipe and slowly filled and lit it.

"I think we'd better get one or two things straight," he said quietly. "What happened a year ago wasn't altogether to my liking—and that includes the part you two played in those events. But it's past history. We all agreed about that before planning this trip. This isn't the time or the place to start remembering old grievances."

"I know that," Jess replied, "but why do we have to stop here? This is where it started, all the killing."

"Then it's a good place for it to finish."

"Isn't there somewhere else?"

"I'm afraid not. The troop you're after spends most of its time deep in the valley. This is the farthest they ever come north, and then only because of the good water. As you've refused to track them down there, we have only one alternative: to stay here. Unless you want to go home. It's up to you."

So in the end they stayed, setting up camp on the spot where the Hunter and his two companions had once waited in ambush.

This particular wait was a lengthy one. For two days there was no sign of the troop, though David and Jess were far from bored during that time. Throughout the daylight hours there was a constant succession of animals coming down to the water to drink; and at night they had Simon's stories of the bush to listen to.

It was on their third evening, sitting peacefully around the camp fire, that David raised an issue that had been worrying him for months.

"How safe is the troop now?" he asked.

Simon took his pipe from his mouth and gazed thoughtfully at the stars overhead.

"As safe as they can ever be in a place like this. Provided they don't raid the farms up above, they shouldn't be bothered by human beings for some years."

"Does that mean they'll be hunted eventually?" Jess broke in. "The way they were by the Hunter that night?"

Simon tended the fire before replying.

"What took place that night," he said at last, "was in my opinion both ill-timed and overdone. But it was right in one respect. The troop had grown too large. Sooner or later it would have been culled anyway, to prevent an overpopulation problem."

"Can't animals be left to work out problems like that for themselves," David asked, "without our shooting them?"

"You can leave them to starve, if that's what you mean," Simon countered, "but I promise you, that's a long and painful business. Bullets aren't nice things, but

213

at least they're quick and efficient. If you were a baboon, which would you prefer?"

They didn't answer, his words reminding them anew of the true nature of this world into which they had ventured, its strange mixture of beauty and harshness, of freedom and peril. Looking past the fire at the surrounding shadows, they could not help but recall the snarl of the leopard and the piercing scream of death in the darkness. Yet as against that terrible moment, there were also vivid memories of Papio and Upi's gentle caresses, of the young baboons, carefree and agile, tumbling together in the shade of the giant fig tree.

"I don't understand any of it," Jess muttered, shaking her head in the same puzzled way as Papio had once shaken his, when he had been faced with the intractable mesh of the enclosure.

But it was as well that they were reminded of the harsh and puzzling quality of their environment, because on the following day the troop arrived. There were furtive movements in the thick bush on the far side of the pool, and then a huge male baboon came sidling out onto the sand. Any doubts as to his identity were dispelled by the sudden bright glint of metal on the top of his head. He moved cautiously to the water's edge, his small eyes flicking this way and that as he searched the bush for hints of danger. Convinced that all was well, he gave a deep satisfied grunt, and other gray-brown shapes emerged behind him, quickly fanning out around the curved rim of the pool.

The troop was now about thirty strong, many of them either babies or juveniles. There was no sign of Ma, though Cyclops had survived, his one blank eye marking him off from the rest. But even without his disability he would have been no match for Papio, who now possessed the same austere majesty that had once characterized Sultan. Restless, powerful, alert, he was the natural leader, guarding the troop with a jealous and loving authority.

"Do you think he still remembers us?" Jess murmured.

She turned questioningly to David, saw the suppressed emotion written clearly on his face.

"I'm sure he couldn't have forgotten completely," he answered.

"Hush," Simon warned them. "You'll scare the whole troop off if you're not careful."

But Jess and David barely heard him.

"There's only one way to find out," Jess said.

David nodded, and together they stood up, in full view of the troop below.

"Papio," David called enticingly, "Papio."

The big leader started up from his drinking posture, standing stiffly on all fours while the other baboons scurried for safety.

"Papio"—Jess softly echoing David's call.

Still on all fours, he was backing away across the sand, deliberately remaining in the open, in a position of danger, until the rest of the troop had gained the shelter of the bush.

"It's us! Jess! David!"

At the sound of those once familiar names, Papio seemed to pause, to falter in mid stride, just for an instant. It was the briefest possible hesitation, soon past. Then he reared defiantly, his mantle fully raised, and roared loudly at them before vanishing into the undergrowth.

"Did you see that?" David burst out. "He nearly stopped! He hasn't forgotten, not completely!"

"He still knows us!" Jess cried.

They turned triumphantly to Simon, but the tall ranger, crouching silently in the background, appeared unmoved by their excitement.

"He didn't look too friendly to me," he said quietly. "As far as I could see, he ran off just like any other wild baboon."

"That's where you're wrong!" David began hotly. "He loves . . . used to love us . . . once . . . when Upi . . . Upi . . ."

As the painful, guilty memories of the past flooded back, he turned and stared out over the now deserted pool. There was a long uncomfortable silence during which the hot stillness of the bush seemed to intensify around them—the even whir of insects, the soothing call of bush doves on the nearby slope, all momentarily blotted out. Jess reached out hesitantly, somehow stretching across the unnatural silence, and touched David's arm.

"Simon's right," she said, her voice hardly more than a whisper. "Papio would never come to us again. He's a wild animal now." David didn't answer, his shoulders hunched and tense, and she added uncertainly: "Isn't that what we were trying to achieve? Really and truly?"

Gradually the tension flowed out of him.

"I suppose so," he murmured at last. "Yes. To be free. Free of the enclosure. Free of . . . of . . . everything."

"Including us?"

"Yes, us too."

David was looking at her now.

"It's like something you mentioned in the Land Rover coming here," she reminded him.

"What was that?"

"About paying for one another's freedom."

He nodded. "Yes, that's about it."

Not without regret they turned their backs on the pool, on the footprints still deeply etched in the sand, and began helping Simon clear up the campsite in preparation for the return journey. It didn't take long, and they were just shouldering their packs when, from far down the valley, there came a muffled bark. They both stood motionless and listened. As though for their special benefit, the bark was repeated. Papio—they were certain of that—calling to them for the last time. Except that now his cry no longer sounded accusing or defiant, to either of them. It had more the quality of a simple, brief farewell.

"Listen to him," David said ruefully, "he hasn't a care in the world." Then with a sudden rush of feeling: "You know something, Jess? I'm glad he's the way he is, wild, out there on his own. Really glad."

A quick look of understanding passed between them.

"Yes," she answered, speaking with a sense of conviction that surprised even herself, "so am I."

AUTHOR'S NOTE

Anyone with a knowledge of Central Africa will recognize, I am sure, that part of the country in which this story is set and also the fact that I have taken some liberties with the geography of the region. What I have tried to achieve is not an exact description of the Zambezi escarpment, but rather a sense of what it feels like to travel through such wild, hilly terrain. To this extent at least, my setting is "true to life."

Much the same holds for my treatment of wild baboons. Wherever possible, my descriptions of baboon behavior are strictly accurate. But probably no one could say for certain how baboons would react to some of the situations described in the preceding pages; and so, from time to time, I had no option but to rely on my own invention. These inventions are not, I hope, too farfetched. Within their native environment baboons are truly remarkable animals—intelligent, courageous, community-minded, and marvelously skilled in the business of survival. It is this larger image of baboons, and not just a series of agreed-upon scientific "facts," that I have attempted to convey.

One final point. The hunting scenes in this book are not merely inventions of mine. I wish they were. Distressingly, baboons have been and, to the best of my knowledge, continue to be hunted in the ways I have described.

Victor Kelleher